Pulphouse

FICTION MAGAZINE

Issue Thirty-Three

I0602693

Magazine Editor

Dean Wesley Smith

A WMG Publishing Magazine

Pulphouse Fiction Magazine Issue #33
Published by WMG Publishing Inc.

Pulphouse

FICTION MAGAZINE

TABLE OF CONTENTS

Pulphouse Fiction Magazine
A WMG Publishing Magazine

Editor	*Executive Editor*	*Director of Operations*
Dean Wesley Smith	**Kristine Kathryn Rusch**	**Stephanie Writt**

FROM THE EDITOR'S DESK
PROMOTION

Some of you may have noticed that some authors have ads for their books and websites and such placed at some point in their story in this magazine.

We offer it to the authors for free and is something that we used to do when we started this magazine. We are finally getting back to it now, among other things that got pushed aside.

We want to help the authors in their business in any small way that we can, and we figure that if a reader likes a story, an ad for the author's work right there with the story might help a little.

As I write this in July, we just finished the Pulphouse Magazine Subscription Drive 2024 Kickstarter. It did really well and we have a good jump on 2024/25 run of this magazine. But we can always use more help and we have wonderful books and products for sale on Pulphouse-Magazine.com.

And we have ads now in this magazine as well to subscribe to Pulphouse or get fun merchandise.

In this new world of publishing, writers are turning to Kickstarters more and more these days to start the promotions of their books, offer fun stuff to their fans, and make some money from their writing early on. And at Pulphouse we like to help the writers where we can.

Let me give you an example…New York Times bestselling writer Kevin J. Anderson had a Dan Shamble: Zombie P.I Adventure in Issue #31 just two issues ago.

He wrote me and told me he is planning a Dan Shamble Kickstarter for the new Dan Shamble novel and was thinking of writing another short story to fill out a collection he would have available in the campaign. He asked me if I would be interested in another Dan Shamble story?

I laughed and said, "Of course, twist my arm."

His Dan Shamble series is a fan favorite in this magazine and always perfect "Pulphouse" stories. In other words they are always stunningly well written, weird as hell, and laugh-out-loud funny. A Zombie P.I.? How is that for mixing genres?

So he wrote the story, I bought it for this issue, of course, and the story will be in a Dan Shamble collection in a month or so after this issue comes out when the Dan Shamble Kickstarter launches.

So make sure you read the story here, along with the other great stories included in this volume. And check out the author's ads for their other work.

And then this fall watch for the Dan Shamble Kickstarter so you can get not only the collection, but also the new Dan Shamble novel.

Have I said before how much I love this new world of publishing?

DEAN WESLEY SMITH
LAS VEGAS, NEVADA

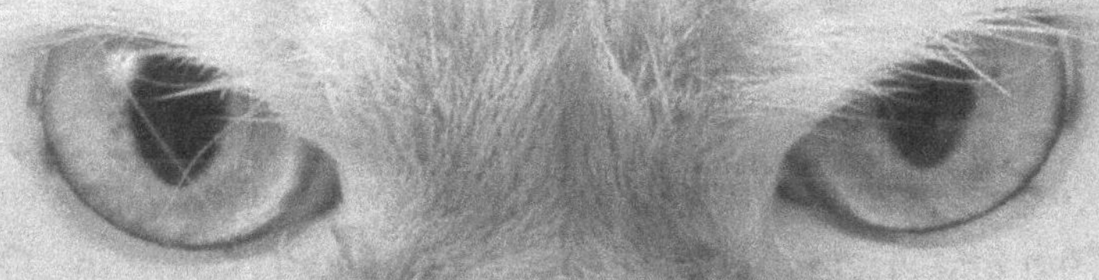

KEVIN J. ANDERSON

Kevin J. Anderson returns for the 15th time to these pages with a really fun and original Dan Shamble, Zombie PI Adventure. Of all the ongoing characters being published these days, Dan Shamble fits Pulphouse the best.

Kevin has published more than 140 bestselling novels and with his wife, bestselling writer Rebecca Moesta, founded Wordfire Press.

Kevin is known for Star Wars, X-Files, *and* Dune *novels, as well as his many original science fiction novels. Back in 2012 he started something a little different for him, a series of humorous horror mysteries featuring Dan Shamble, Zombie P.I.*

Watch for the new Dan Shamble novel in a Kickstarter coming this fall.

I just love the fact that we have Dan Shamble in these pages.

HOLY BALLS
A DAN SHAMBLE, ZOMBIE P.I. ADVENTURE
KEVIN J. ANDERSON

One

"You hold my balls in your hands," said the warlock. I could tell from his expression he was uneasy. "Take good care of them."

Actually, his balls were much too large to fit in my palms. "They're bigger than I expected," I said. "Put them on the table and let's have a look."

The warlock's name was Vincent, an older, wiry man who looked scrawny but not the least bit frail. He was bald, with a prominent Adam's apple on his long neck, and a narrow gray beard that hung like a dribbly waterfall of whiskers from the point of his chin. He reminded me of a cartoon wizard, though he insisted that warlocks were different from wizards. (As a zombie private investigator, I accept any and all kinds of clients.)

With a grunt of effort, Vincent set the first of the two large crystal balls on the display in our front office. I moved some old magazines aside to make room for the other ball. The second transparent orb looked identical to the first.

"I need your security expertise, Mr. Shamble." The warlock drew his bushy gray eyebrows together. "No one can see what's in these crystal balls—especially not my nosy wife." Vincent flicked his eyes back and forth, as if his head were filled with guilty secrets.

"I normally work as a detective," I told him, "but we also provide security services. I have a gun license and a P.I. license." Mollified, Vincent peered down into the pair of crystalline spheres. He had already met with my human lawyer partner, Robin Deyer, the week before to discuss the matter with her, and now he was back to see me.

"Tell me exactly what you're looking for, sir," I said, "and we'll take care of it."

At Chambeaux & Deyer Investigations, we solve crimes and handle legal matters for naturals and unnaturals. Robin is a fierce defender of unnatural rights in court, and I often wander the Unnatural Quarter in search of clues.

"I am a powerful warlock, as you see." Vincent spread his arms. He wore a black velvet robe with embroidered stars, crescent moons, and strange constellation diagrams. "And I can predict the future by gazing into my sacred crystal ball."

"I'm familiar with the concept," I said. "I had a magic eight-ball once."

"My wife, Dismerelda, is also a fortune-teller and future-predictor, but she prefers to use tarot cards. We both have a very similar magical skill set, but we don't perform tricks. We predict the future. We're prognosticators, not prestidigitators.

And we aren't ridiculous frauds like those scam telepsychics who advertise on billboards across the city."

"I've never used one of those services, nor do I intend to." I had always been skeptical about psychic hotlines and fortune-tellers—but that was before the Big Uneasy, the event that returned all ghosts, mummies, werewolves, vampires, and other mythical creatures to the world. When you see monsters shambling around every day, it's hard to be skeptical about much of anything anymore.

"Good," Vincent said. "Always use real magic, I say."

I ran my palm over the nearest crystal ball, expecting sparkles, but nothing happened—not even a little flurry of white flecks, like from a snow globe. "So a witch and a warlock—you sound like a perfect couple."

He gazed down at the identical crystal balls. "We've been married for twenty years. Our anniversary is coming up." His expression suddenly hardened. "Dismerelda's a powerful witch, and I never underestimate her abilities—or her deviousness. You must keep her from looking into my crystal ball!"

"And why are there two of them?"

"One of these is a decoy—a distraction to help you keep the real one safe." Vincent waved his hand over the two spheres. "Dismerelda is always snooping and prying, digging into my private affairs, putting her nose where it doesn't belong." He raised his eyebrows. "Did I mention we've been married twenty years?"

"It's hard to imagine you still have secrets from her after all that time," I said.

"That's exactly the problem! She pries into everything. And sometimes, a man needs to have secrets, you know."

Sheyenne, my beautiful poltergeist girlfriend, drifted over from the reception desk to see if she could help us. I knew she had also been eavesdropping. "What sort of secrets, Vincent?"

"They're a secret!" he said. "I caught Dismerelda eyeing my balls the other day, trying to stare into the future to find what I'd been doing and what I was thinking. Fortunately, I caught her in time and covered them up. If she gets her hands on these, she'll ruin everything. I need you, Mr. Shamble, to keep these crystal balls under lock and key." He picked up the nearest one, hefted it in his hands, and passed it to me. It was much heavier than I thought.

"This one is a decoy. Lock it in your safe and make sure everyone knows you're guarding it there." He gestured to the second holy ball. "Then quietly hide the other in an even better place. I'll pay you handsomely to keep the real one safe and out of Dismerelda's view for one week. After that, it won't matter."

Vincent removed two large black fabric bags from a pocket in his warlock robe. "Here, keep each one hidden and protected in this special ball sack—and be very gentle with them."

— — —

Two

SOMETIMES IN THE UNNATURAL QUARTER, THE DAYS NEVER seem to end. But when I can end the day with a cold beer at the Goblin Tavern, then I call it a good day.

Today was a good day.

"Hey, McGoo," I said as I climbed stiffly onto my usual bar stool. Officer Toby McGoohan, my best human friend, had a fresh beer in front of him. He wore his blue patrolman's uniform; his cap was on the bar beside him.

"Hey, Shamble," he said. "Do you know why a mummy movie director always finishes a scene on time? Because he can't wait to shout 'It's a wrap!'"

He knew I wouldn't laugh. "My new client is a warlock, says he can predict the future. I'll ask him to predict when you'll tell a joke that's funny."

McGoo snorted and slurped his beer. "I like to be unpredictable."

I waved for Francine, the hard-bitten human bartender who was tough enough to put up with any sort of monster customer. Because I was a regular, she was already filling a pint of my favorite beer. When she delivered it, she looked at the two of us. "Next time you bring in that little vampire girl of yours, I'll teach her how to make a Roy Jugular. That's her drink of choice, right?"

I nodded. "It's what Alvina orders every time we come in here."

"I have a special recipe for special customers," Francine said. "That squirt has potential. If she plays her cards right, she could be a bartender someday."

"She does like to mix weird chemicals for her mad scientist chemistry lab experiments at school," I said.

McGoo agreed as he sipped his beer. "We want to make sure Al is equipped with life skills."

I took a long drink and let out a satisfied sigh. Once I transformed into a zombie, my sense of taste sucks, but drinking beer was an old social habit and it felt good going down cold. "Any big cases today, McGoo?"

He shrugged. "It's been quiet in the Quarter all week. The worst I'm dealing with is some vandalism on those new telepsychic billboards. Big spray-painted words. 'Fraud!' And 'Bet you didn't predict this graffiti.'"

"Probably just zombie slackers," I said.

"Not zombies," McGoo said. "The spelling was good, and they finished all the letters instead of just petering out as they lost their train of thought."

At a table in back next to the pool table, five dusty old mummies, a college fraternity group I think, were engaged in a drinking game while a scorekeeper wrote painstakingly detailed hieroglyphics on a scratch pad.

Two other fraternity mummies were engaged in an arm-wrestling contest. The bandage-wrapped skeletal figures clutched hands, rested elbows on the tabletop, and strained, clenching their sinewy jaws as they pushed harder and harder. When I heard a loud, hollow *crack*, I cringed. The rowdy mummies scrambled to get out fresh linens to bandage up the break.

Suddenly at the front door of the Goblin Tavern, a swirling cloud of emerald green smoke erupted, as if someone had just cracked open a gas grenade. The smoke billowed upward, smelling strongly of cabbage, and I heard a shrill cackle of laughter. Emerging from the swirl of smoke was a gaunt, greenish-skinned witch in a pointy black hat and a black dress. She had a long, bent chin and an equally long and bent nose, both of which held prominent warts. She cackled and shrieked again as she looked around with blazing green eyes.

Everyone in the tavern turned to her, waiting in anticipation for something interesting to happen. The mummy fraternity group even stopped their game. The witch shouted, "Where's Dan Chambeaux? I've got business with him!"

Francine, McGoo, and many of the other bar patrons swung their gazes toward me. "At least she wants to talk business," I told McGoo. I raised my gray hand, since there was no way to duck out of this.

The witch stalked over like a battering ram. Her black dress swished and swirled. Her pointed nose and chin looked like dangerous weapons. "You've got something of mine!"

"At the moment, I don't even have your name," I said, wondering what this was about.

"I'm Dismerelda. I want that crystal ball. Give it to me!"

"Actually, it's your husband's ball," I said.

"Community property!" she snapped.

"You've got her husband's balls?" McGoo said.

I flicked him an annoyed look. "That's an obvious joke, McGoo, but I thought you'd like it."

He chuckled and drank his beer.

"Your husband engaged my services to hold the crystal ball for safekeeping, and he specifically wants me to keep it away from you."

"Where is it?"

"Locked in a completely safe place." I knew I had to be firm. "I cannot help you, ma'am. The crystal ball belongs to Vincent."

Anger flared on Dismerelda's face. "You'll be sorry for that! I'll make you pay."

"Your husband is paying. Quite substantially." I crossed my arms over my chest, standing tough against this demanding witch. Zombies can be implacable.

"I need to see what's in that crystal ball. I need to know his secret!"

"If you had a solid marriage, you could just discuss that

with him," I pointed out. I knew that's what Sheyenne would have said.

"A solid marriage? We've been married twenty years!"

"He told me. Congratulations," I said, then hardened my voice again. "But I can't give you the crystal ball. Period."

In a huff, the witch swirled around and stalked back toward the door, which she flung open. Outside, against the wall of the Goblin Tavern, she had propped a long broom with a padded broomstick. "We're not finished with this, Dan Chambeaux!"

She hurled out another smokescreen of green, roiling vapors, which didn't entirely obscure her exit. She hopped on the broom and flew off into the dark, gloomy skies of the Unnatural Quarter.

McGoo and I ordered another beer.

Three

The following afternoon, Sheyenne and I met young Alvina after Nosferatu Academy let out for the day. The kid was perfectly capable of walking home all by herself, but we enjoyed the company.

The little vampire girl was cute as a button, with her blond hair tied into two pigtails, a pleated plaid skirt from school, her favorite fuzzy pink sweater, and her unicorn backpack. If any unnatural tried to harass her, I pitied them. She would flash her little baby fangs, and if that wasn't threatening enough, she would kick them in the gonads. For a school paper, she had researched the vulnerable testicular areas of various unnatural creatures, or the equivalent spots in asexual entities.

McGoo and I didn't know which of us was the real father of the kid, who had been turned into a vampire after a botched blood transfusion. Her mother had had a fling with both of us at about the same time, and then she had dumped the girl on us when she couldn't handle caring for an unnatural daughter. McGoo and I didn't mind. We adored Alvina and took turns watching her.

"So how was school today, honey?" Sheyenne asked.

"Lots of fun," Alvina said with a bright smile. "We're having a comparative apocalypse unit. It's called 'What's the worst that could happen?'"

"I like it when you're optimistic, kid." I tousled her hair, making the pigtails jiggle.

On the night of the Big Uneasy, when twisted magic had unleashed every legendary creature, people had thought *that* was the end of the world, but we got over it just fine. It only took a few years for people to realize that the world hadn't actually turned into a horror movie, but was more like an everyday sitcom, just with an additional cast of characters.

At Chambeaux & Deyer, we had plenty of job security. Unnaturals still got divorced, still got involved in petty crimes or frivolous lawsuits. As a lawyer, Robin had decided to focus on finding justice for underserved unnaturals. I was a human private investigator and had worked cases for many unnaturals, until I got shot in the back of the head. But thanks to the new rules, I had returned as a zombie and clawed my way out of the grave—back from the dead, and back on the case.

Just before I was killed, Sheyenne had been a medical student moonlighting as a cocktail waitress and lounge singer at the Basilisk Nightclub. We'd had a short but passionate relationship, and then she was poisoned to death on the same case that got me killed. She returned as a ghost instead of a zombie, but we were still a couple.

Now, we had light, comfortable conversation as we walked along the main boulevard. Vincent's sacred crystal ball decoy was securely locked in the office safe, which was the most obvious place I could think of to store it. And I'd hidden the other one, the real one, upstairs in my own small dingy apartment, wrapped in its ball sack and rolled in blankets inside the cardboard air-conditioner box that Alvina used as her coffin when she slept over.

Today the Quarter was active with local street vendors: a tentacle creature showing off with hacky sacks, a banshee with a boombox trying to sell her CDs. At a Talbot & Knowles blood bar we bought Alvina one of her favorite unicorn frappés, because I knew the sugar rush would give her the energy to do her homework.

Surprisingly, we came upon a table with a familiar warlock and witch sitting next to each other, stiff-backed and cold-shouldered. A handwritten poster board said, "Fortunes told and contradicted. Know your future, believe it or not." A large jar sat between Vincent and Dismerelda holding loose change. It reminded me of a lemonade stand that Alvina had wanted to set up.

"Can I get my fortune told?" Alvina said. "I always wanted a fortune."

"It probably costs a fortune," Sheyenne said.

Vincent and Dismerelda both saw me at the same time, but then pivoted to stare at Alvina, their target. "Know your future, little girl?" Dismerelda cackled.

"I have a bright future," Alvina said. "Is this a scam?"

The warlock and the witch both raised their chins, making similar movements like a long-married couple. "Our prognostication is real," Vincent said.

The witch added, "Not like those fake telepsychics who don't know what they're doing."

At the mention of telepsychics, both Vincent and Dismerelda turned to opposite sides of the table and spat on the sidewalk in disgust.

"I'm surprised to see you here together," I said.

"We've got to make a living," Vincent said. "Don't we, dear?"

Turning away from him with an annoyed sniff, Dismerelda said, "My husband can't help you, because he doesn't have his crystal ball today. You'll have to trust my sacred tarot cards."

Dismerelda pulled out a pack of tarot cards and spread

them on the table. As Alvina watched with intense curiosity, the witch laid out the cards in a specific pattern, flipping them over one at a time, then she looked up at Alvina with a deeply troubled expression. "You have a very dark future, little girl. I fear that you may go into ... politics."

Alvina brightened. "I could be the mayor of the Unnatural Quarter."

Vincent huffed. "Dismerelda always gets it wrong, because she doesn't have my holy crystal ball. Here, let me tell your correct fortune." He reached into a brown paper bag next to him and pulled out a handful of plastic-wrapped Chinese fortune cookies. "These are never wrong." He spread the wrapped cookies on the table and gestured Alvina closer. "Pick one, child. You will know your own fortune."

Alvina slurped on her unicorn frappé, then snatched one of the cookies.

"Now, open it up and reveal your true destiny," Vincent said.

She unwrapped the cookie and cracked it open. The warlock took the little tag of paper and perused it in deep concentration. "Ah, yes. I know this is accurate. Today you will meet someone interesting."

She looked at the warlock. "You're interesting."

"Fortune cookies never lie," Vincent said. "And I can go into more detail once I have my crystal ball back in a few days."

Alvina took even greater pleasure eating the sweet crunchy cookie. "Maybe I'll go into politics, or chemistry. But right now, I'm a private investigator's research assistant."

"You can be anything you want, honey," Sheyenne said.

As we continued along, Vincent called after us. "Protect my holy possessions, Mr. Shamble."

I took my job seriously. "It's locked up tight in the safe in our offices, sir. No one can get to it."

Dismerelda remained icily angry at her husband and didn't say a word.

Four

LATE AT NIGHT, THE UNNATURAL QUARTER IS REALLY HOPPING, but I felt tired. McGoo was watching Alvina (she has an identical empty air-conditioner box for a sleepover coffin at his place), so he and I didn't meet up at the Goblin Tavern as usual. After working hard on some court filings, Robin had gone home.

Sheyenne and I went out for a nice drink and conversation at her old haunt, the Basilisk Nightclub, and we came back to the dark and empty offices long after midnight—and came upon a violent burglary in progress.

I immediately knew something was wrong when I saw our office door ajar. I gestured Sheyenne to stay behind me for safety, although that was just an instinctive gesture, because nothing much could harm a poltergeist. She glided past me through the wall, while I pushed open the door.

Inside, I spotted the large rolling garbage can, the steel bucket with gray water and pungent pine-smelling solvent, and the erect mop handle. I realized that we had simply interrupted the Bigfoot janitorial crew. We had hired the cleaning service to add a little extra sparkle to the office. Though Bigfeet were large and hairy and tended to leave footprints everywhere, they were quiet, unobtrusive, and rarely seen, and thus made perfect janitorial staff. I hardly ever noticed them myself.

Now, though, I spotted the tall hairy creature clutching his push broom and standing against the wall, terrified, his large eyes wide, his big fanged mouth open with gibbering fear.

A green ectoplasmic entity, like a terrifying knot of poisonous vapor, was swirling around our steel office safe. The Bigfoot let out a grunt of terror. The green smoke churned and flailed—and I watched the safe's combination wheel spinning and whirling back and forth, back and forth, trying thousands of different combinations, one after another, like a computer algorithm made out of fumes.

"Hey, stop that!" I shouted.

The smoke redoubled its efforts, and with a *click-clunk*, somehow stumbled upon the right combination. The heavy, steel door of the safe swung open.

Sheyenne drifted forward. "Don't you dare!"

But the roiling cloud entered the open cavity of the safe and grabbed the wizard's ball sack. Sheyenne floated in front of it, trying to stop the theft, but the green smoke and the heavy bag pushed right through her spectral form.

I grabbed the push broom from the terrified Bigfoot janitor and swept at the fumes, but the floating black bag struck me in the head like a bowling ball, and knocked my fedora askew. The cloud of smoke roiled and pummeled past me, then whooshed out into the hall. I staggered after the fleeing criminal vapors, but the smoke picked up speed, and the dangling ball sack swung back and forth.

Sheyenne rushed up to me as the felonious fumes hurtled down the stairs and out of the building. "Are you all right, Beaux? That looked like a hard blow."

"I've got a thick skull," I said, "and there's not much in it. I'm okay."

As we watched the greenish smoke disappear, I straightened my fedora, just because it helped restore my self-confidence. "At least that was just the decoy. Vincent gave it to me for a reason. Maybe that'll keep the witch off track."

Sheyenne was clearly angry. "Do you think that was Dismerelda? She looked different at the prognostication stand."

"She's involved at least. The green smoke is sort of her signature move." I went over to the open door of the safe. "But she left no fingerprints and no identifying features, so we can't prove anything."

Behind us, the Bigfoot was discreetly finishing up his janitorial duties. We hardly noticed him.

"Get me Vincent's number, Spooky," I said. "I'd better call him."

When I told the warlock our dire news, he actually cackled with a sound much like his wife's. "Ha! I knew she would try something like that! She just couldn't resist the temptation. I told her to leave it alone, but that just made her more angry. Oh, she'll learn her lesson soon enough."

"Sorry I let you down, Vincent. I thought our office safe was secure. It was the highest-rated model on Amazon."

"Never trust those ratings," Vincent said. "But it doesn't matter. You just need to keep the real one absolutely, positively safe. For another four days."

Five

AFTER DISMERELDA HAD BEEN FOILED BY THE DECOY CRYSTAL ball, she tried an even more devious and underhanded tactic to get what she wanted.

She hired a lawyer.

Fortunately, the lawyer was our own Robin Deyer, which kept the situation simple, straightforward, and incredibly complicated. If Vincent had still possessed his holy ball, he might have foreseen the complication, but his fortune cookies were inadequate to the task.

Dismerelda flung open the door and stood there so we could take in the threat. In her pointed hat and black traditional dress, she carried her broomstick upright as she stalked into the office, then thrust the stick into our umbrella stand, where it rested against the wall. The witch always seemed to make a grand entrance. She would have done well if she tried out for the lead role in an Unnatural Quarter revival of *Wicked.*

"I'm here to see Robin Deyer, Esquire. I intend to engage her services—I hear she always wins." Dismerelda raised her crooked, warty chin and made a sniff through her crooked, warty nose.

Robin emerged from her office and regarded the witch. "I always win when the cause is just."

"Well, my cause is just *desserts,*" she snapped. "I need to get what is mine—my husband's secrets. We share everything, but he won't share whatever he's hiding from me. And I must have it. I'll sue!" She held up a black clutch purse and opened it. "Let me pay your retainer, Ms. Deyer, so we can get started right away."

Robin was cool and discomfited, but I had already risen to a level of pissed off. "You couldn't get what you desired through illegal means, so now you're trying legal means?"

Dismerelda's wart jiggled on her nostril. "I have no idea what you mean."

Sheyenne sat indignant at her reception desk. "You broke in here last night. You cracked our safe, and you stole the crystal ball."

"Prove it," Dismerelda said. "Do you have any photographs? Any fingerprints? Any witnesses that can identify me?"

I spoke up. "We saw a nasty clot of green smoke. That reminded me of you, distinctly."

Robin pressed her lips together in a hard line. "It won't hold up in court, Dan, even if we know she did it."

"That fake crystal ball held no value whatsoever. It was as ridiculous as a telepsychic." Dismerelda leaned to one side and spat on our carpet.

I would have to make a note for the Bigfoot janitor to clean that spot. Carefully.

The witch continued, "I want to sue for possession of my husband's crystal ball. It is community property. His secrets are my secrets, and I need to see what he doesn't want me to see."

"There's a conflict of interest," Robin said. "We already represent your husband. I cannot represent you on the opposing side."

Dismerelda held up a gnarled finger. "Vincent hired Dan Chambeaux for security services. I intend to hire you for legal services. Completely different."

"That's not how it works, ma'am," Robin said. "I can reference any number of legal tomes."

Even I knew that the witch had a losing argument, but I could tell from her demeanor that losing wasn't going to stop her from arguing.

We were saved, or at least distracted, by the arrival of the warlock. Vincent stalked in, thrusting out his chin to waggle his long, gray waterfall of beard. While Dismerelda seemed outraged and indignant, Vincent was amused. His eyes sparkled. "Now, my dear, you've never been good at admitting defeat, and you just can't leave well enough alone. If you loved me, you would trust me."

I thought the witch was going to snatch up her broom and sweep the amused expression off his face. "I can't trust you when I know you're keeping secrets. What are you hiding? You're sneaking around behind my back."

Vincent crossed his arms over his black warlock's robe. "No, my dear, I am sneaking around right in front of your face, and you just can't stand it."

He chuckled, which only enraged his wife more. "You tricked me with that fake crystal ball. Where is the real one? I want it back now. I'll sue!"

Sheyenne rose up, glowing. "Could I get anyone coffee? Or water?"

Unruffled, Robin stepped in between them with a calm, businesslike demeanor. "That's enough talk about lawsuits from both of you. I'm always an advocate of talking matters through. I would suggest an arbitration conference, so we can discuss how to satisfy both of you."

"I'll be satisfied when I have his balls firmly back in my hands," Dismerelda said.

"You need to learn a little patience, my dear," Vincent said. "You never know what surprises are in store."

"I don't like surprises," Dismerelda said.

"And that's no surprise to me," he countered, "which is why you make this so difficult." He turned to Robin, sounding very reasonable. "I'll agree to an arbitration conference. Let's schedule something for…." He paused, touched a finger to his lower lip. "Three days from now."

That was when his contract with us ended. Even though he was a paying client, I was going to be happy to roll these balls out of our lives.

Dismerelda considered. "I have a Pointy Hat Society luncheon in two days, but that time frame seems clear to me. As long as we can resolve this—in my favor."

Vincent was smiling, his eyes sparkling, and Sheyenne put the meeting on the calendar.

Six

FULLY AWARE OF THE EXTREME MEASURES DISMERELDA WAS willing to take, I redoubled my efforts to guard the real crystal ball. We'd made no secret, on purpose, that Vincent's decoy had been stored in our office safe, but nobody knew the other hiding place. I worried, though, that Dismerelda could use wily magical means—whether through tarot cards or fortune cookies or something even more esoteric—to figure out where I'd hidden the real crystal ball. Talented prognosticators can be unpredictable.

Wrapping the glass sphere in Alvina's unicorn blanket then stuffing it inside her coffin air-conditioner box seemed like a brilliant trick, but I would also rely on brute force. For the last couple of days when the crystal ball was in my care, I vowed not to let it out of my sight.

For the time being, McGoo watched over Alvina when she wasn't in school. I didn't imagine that Dismerelda would genuinely threaten our vampire girl, but I wasn't going to risk putting her in danger.

That night, I sat upstairs with my .38 in hand, completely alert. I was going to be a restless zombie until this was all over. I sat hunched in my own chair next to the air-conditioner box after double-checking that the hiding place was safe and secure. I even fondled the ball sack to make sure the precious magical item was still there.

I watched the seconds tick by on the clock on the wall, tense, alert, and determined.

Sheyenne made the stakeout more than tolerable, pleasant even. I smiled at her glowing presence in the room with me. "You can keep me company any day or any night, Spooky."

"I'm cheaper than a regular security guard," she said.

"And less at risk," I replied. Security guards in a city full of monsters didn't tend to fare well.

I thought of the good times we'd had together, even though our relationship as humans had been all too brief. She'd been so beautiful singing on the Basilisk stage. I was smitten with her the first time she crooned out "Spooky," and that had become our signature song.

Now as we hung out, watchful against any malevolent clouds of aggressive green smoke, Sheyenne grew contemplative. "Those two have been married for so long, Beaux. The witch and the warlock seem to have so much in common. Looking at the shine in Vincent's eyes, I can tell he cares for Dismerelda."

"He cares for his secrets even more, though," I said. "But he was right in what he said today. If she trusted him, it wouldn't be such a big deal."

"What if his secret is something terrible?" she asked. "What do you think Vincent is hiding from her?"

"We don't know it's terrible," I said. "Could be just something he doesn't want her to know."

I wondered how I would feel if someone else could see my every action, every thought, every embarrassing moment or confidential activity.

"So would you ever keep secrets from me?" she asked.

I was about to make a joke, but I saw the expression on her face and knew I needed to take it seriously. "Spooky, we've been together long enough. I don't have any secrets from you." I tapped my head, and the bullet hole there made a hollow sound in my skull. "You can look inside anytime you want."

She leaned over to give me a glowing ectoplasmic kiss. "I know you've got nothing to hide."

<hr>

Seven

I DIDN'T NEED A CRYSTAL BALL TO PREDICT THAT THE arbitration meeting was going to be tense. Frankly, I'd be glad to wrap up the case and get rid of the problematic magical artifact. Let Vincent the warlock handle his own balls from now on.

I always say the cases don't solve themselves, but this hadn't been a mystery—just a pain-in-the-butt security matter.

Robin had handled unnatural divorces, prenuptial agreements, transformative bonds, and custody agreements after love spells wore off. She knew all the law's fine points about community property, whether with mundane objects or powerful cursed artifacts.

Dismerelda's indignation seemed to go beyond any statutes and codes.

We sat at the conference table with Vincent on one end and his witch wife glowering at him from the other. The warlock remained stony-faced, a closed book, but I sensed a building anticipation, as if he was clutching a secret about his own secrets.

Robin produced a yellow legal pad and her ensorcelled pencil for taking notes. "Now then, shall we begin?"

"We can begin by bringing the real crystal ball here," Dismerelda said. "You, Mr. Shamble—go upstairs and get it from where you've hidden it."

I held up my gray hands. "I never said where the real crystal ball is. What makes you think it's upstairs?"

"I am a prognosticator." Dismerelda crossed her arms over her black dress. "I know things."

Vincent let out a hard chuckle. "You don't know everything, my dear."

The witch stabbed a gnarled greenish finger at me, and I

saw that she'd put on a fresh coat of black nail polish. "You tricked me with a false crystal ball in your safe, but I know that the real one is somewhere else, somewhere close." She closed her eyes, concentrating. "The other ball is hidden in a...coffin, or a box. And I sense a blanket, a unicorn blanket."

For a moment I couldn't find words. Sheyenne hovered next to me, and we both exchanged an alarmed glance. "That's pretty good," I said.

Vincent was offended. "You learned all that from your tarot cards, my dear?"

"You forced me to take desperate measures." The witch sounded embarrassed. "I had to call a telepsychic, and they revealed where it was."

Vincent leaned to one side and spat in disgust, then faced us with a big happy grin. "Ha ha, I knew it! And they were wrong! Even the telepsychic doesn't know where my real crystal ball is."

I was confused. "Well, not exactly wrong...." I looked at Robin. "Uh, should I go upstairs and get it?"

Robin had a strange and uncomfortable expression on her face. "Yes, for the sake of this meeting."

I've known Robin a long time, and I usually know what she's thinking, but this time she was unreadable. Could my own lawyer partner be keeping secrets from her zombie friend?

Dismerelda said, "I'll wait."

Not sure how this would end, I left the conference room and trudged upstairs to my little apartment, where I rummaged in Alvina's cardboard coffin box to retrieve the precious object. Carrying the heavy crystal sphere, I returned downstairs and placed it in the middle of the conference table. I left the black fabric bag cinched closed, though. "It was right where the telepsychic said it would be."

Vincent spat at the side of the table again. "Please don't do that," Sheyenne said. "It's unsanitary."

"I have a right to see the crystal ball," Dismerelda said. "I want to know what my husband is keeping from me. Are you having an affair? Are you addicted to gambling? Do you have an identical twin you never told me about?"

"All in good time, my dear," Vincent said with a sniff. "You are so damned impatient, you make it difficult for me to do my husbandly duties."

The desperate witch surprised us all by snatching the ball sack, using her clawed fingernails to tear open the drawstring. As she yanked out the smooth crystal sphere, Vincent lunged, trying to stop her. "No, not yet!" he said.

But they fumbled the ball. It bounced up and off the edge of the table, then crashed onto the floor. The crystal ball cracked in half, breaking open.

Dismerelda shrieked. "What?"

Vincent chuckled. "You see, it was just a cheap fake."

I glanced at Sheyenne, then Robin. "Wait…it was another decoy?"

Robin stood up, prim and professional. "Dan did not have the real crystal ball. Both were fakes."

I gasped, which is unusual, because I don't breathe much. "Vincent, you told me the one from the safe was a decoy."

The warlock kept grinning. "But I didn't promise the other one was real."

Robin explained, "Vincent came to me the previous week

and contracted my services. I've had the warlock's real crystal ball all this time."

Vincent looked at me and spread his hands apologetically. "I gazed into my crystal ball, Mr. Shamble, and I knew you would fumble the job at least once. I needed to make sure."

Even Sheyenne was astonished. "Where did you keep the real crystal ball?"

Robin walked over to the conference room door. "Right in my desk drawer, where no one would think to look. I'll be back in a minute."

We were surrounded by a great deal of uncomfortable silence, until Robin returned with yet another fabric ball sack. She placed a third crystal ball onto the table, and the warlock gave her a satisfied smile. "You did an admirable job, Ms. Deyer, and your fee is most reasonable. I only needed to keep my crystal ball away from sweet Dismerelda's eyes until today."

"Vincent, you had better explain yourself," the witch warned.

He was beaming. "You have been so obsessed and preoccupied, my dear. I think you've forgotten what today is."

"Today is the day of our arbitration, when I can finally see what secrets you've held in that crystal ball."

He held up a finger and announced, "Today is also our twentieth wedding anniversary."

Sheyenne brightened. "Congratulations to the loving couple."

Vincent unfastened the drawstring on the real ball sack and pushed down the folds of cloth. "I have been planning this for some time, Dismerelda. I wanted to surprise you with a special present—but because you're always so nosy, looking into everything I do, sneaking glimpses into my crystal ball, I had a devil of a time getting you a surprise gift."

The witch fluttered her black-nailed hands in front of her mouth in astonishment. "You got me a gift? I've never been surprised before."

"That's because you always look into my crystal ball," Vincent said. "This took careful planning, believe me." He ran his palms over the smooth, curved glass surface. Glimmers of light and swirls of mist appeared inside. I saw sandy beaches, palm trees.

"What is this, Vincent?" Dismerelda said.

"A second honeymoon for us, a seven-day cruise and a relaxing vacation in the Bahamas."

"The Bahamas?" Dismerelda cried. "I've always wanted to go there."

"Are you surprised?" Now Vincent just sounded smug.

She clutched her hands in front of her chest. "I'm so sorry I doubted you. This is wonderful. I can't believe you did this!"

"You're worth it. You should see the look on your face."

"I...I don't know what to say," Dismerelda said.

"You could say you love me," Vincent said.

She leaned close and rubbed her crooked, warty nose against his cheek. Then they smooched.

Glowing, Sheyenne drifted close to me. "Oh, how romantic."

Robin closed the folders on the table in front of her. "I wish it hadn't escalated so much, but we had to maintain our confidentiality. We're happy to help you accomplish your desire, Vincent."

Still kissing, he and Dismerelda paid little attention to the legal comment.

"You could try to surprise me like that sometime, Beaux," Sheyenne suggested.

"I don't need to keep anything a secret from you," I said. "Besides, I don't think I have the balls for it."

DAVID H. HENDRICKSON

Full-time professional writer David H. Hendrickson has been a writer for many, many years, not only as a fiction writer, but writing thousands of sports articles. He knows writing. And he knows life.

With Dave, you never know what kind of story you will get, which as editor and fan of his work, I love. This story is an example of that, taking something from history (sort of) and putting real people (sort of) in it to make it come alive in a family drama kind of way (sort of).

Dave's short fiction has appeared in Best American Mystery Stories, Ellery Queen's Mystery Magazine, Heart's Kiss, *and numerous anthologies, including over a half dozen issues of* Fiction River *and just about every issue of this magazine so far. Check it all out at http://www.hendricksonwriter.com/*

BELOVED

DAVID H. HENDRICKSON

There's nothing like a man holding the severed head of a giant to get a woman in the mood.

It did nothing for me, but my younger sister, Michal, looked to be in heat. Her pretty little face flushed. Her bosom, more ample than mine, heaved. Her breath came in short, quick gasps.

"He's so handsome," she said.

Atop a platform that overlooked the palace courtyard, David lifted Goliath's head and shook it. The crowd roared. Women danced and beat upon their tambourines. Men still decked out in their battlefield attire raised their spears and shouted. Clouds of dust rose up to us on the royal balcony beside the platform.

"Look at those eyes," Michal gushed.

She was becoming insufferable. "What if the stone missed the giant?" I asked. "Would he still be so handsome? What if he ran from the fight, so terrified he soiled his loincloth? Would his eyes still be so pretty?"

A pout formed on Michal's lips. "You're such a cynic, Merab. There's not a man in Israel that could impress you." She finally tore her eyes away from David. "If Father expects to marry you away first, I might die a virgin."

Father would have no trouble marrying me off; he was the king. But Michal would be the prize. She was the pretty one. I was plain. Serviceable. Like a healthy donkey.

"Maybe I don't want marry," I said.

She shook her head in that way that said she'd never understand me. "Well, I do." Her cheeks burned red. "David, son of Jesse," she said. "I'm going to marry him some day."

I raised my eyebrows. "Does he know?"

"You can be so—"

She gasped and touched my arm. "He's coming this way!"

David strode to our side of the platform, his eyes fixed on Michal. Following behind him were my father, King Saul, and my brother, Jonathan. I'd heard David had been a humble shepherd, but those days were no more. He looked drunk with the glory being showered upon him.

Michal gripped my arm tighter. I thought she might fall over into a dead faint.

David bent one knee and bowed his head. "King Saul's daughters are as fair as this day is great."

A smooth talker. As if Michal weren't already smitten.

"Tell us of your feat, O Champion," she said.

David beamed. "The Lord God Jehovah slew the giant. I was but his instrument."

Clever, I thought. The obligatory deference followed by a proud retelling.

Her voice quivering, Michal asked, "Will you deny the king's daughter your story?"

"Of course not." David smiled. "The giant threatened all of Israel, commanding us to send one man who would fight him. Your father, the King, offered me his armor, helmet, and coat of mail, but I took them off. Instead, I chose five smooth stones from a brook and put one within my sling. The first one struck the giant in the head and he toppled to the ground. I fell upon him and, using his own sword, cut off his head."

David shook the giant's head again, setting off another roar from the crowd.

"This was your first time in battle?" Michal asked.

David flushed.

My sweet, pretty sister had not the sense of the flies buzzing about the giant's head.

"Yes," David said, "but while tending my father's sheep, I defended the flock by killing a lion and a bear with my own hands."

"A lion?" Michal gasped. "And a bear? With your own hands?"

So much, I thought, for deference to the Lord God Jehovah.

"I caught the creature by its beard, struck it, and killed it."

"Such bravery!" Michal said.

I stifled a laugh. If there had been a lion or bear, I was pretty sure that what had protected the flock was a rock within David's sling. There'd been no wrestling the beast to the ground, much less beating it to death with David's bare hands. It was a nice tale to charm the young women of the kingdom, but I didn't believe it.

The way his chest swelled with pride, though, I suspected he'd come to believe the tale himself. Vanity at its worst.

"Your mother, the Queen, awaits our appearance inside the palace," David said. He looked at Michal. "Perhaps we shall meet again."

"Yes," she said, looking as though she might throw herself off the balcony to him.

David bowed and turned away.

For the next few days, every time I spotted Michal with that love-struck look in her eyes, I said, "He's beating another lion to death right now. With his bare hands!" I'd gasp and add, "Such bravery!"

She'd glare or perhaps throw something at me as I burst into laughter, but eventually she began to laugh too.

"He was trying to impress me, that's all," she said. "There's no harm in a little embellishment. He can't be perfect."

"Of course," I said. "Just trying to impress. I'm sure he's as smitten with you as you are with him." Then I mimicked her dreamy-eyed look.

"That's not funny, Merab," she said.

"You should see yourself."

A pout came over her lips. "Will you speak to Father about David for me? He listens to you. He treats me as if I'm still a child."

I gave her the look. "I wonder why."

"I'm a woman now," she said defensively. "Just because you're the eldest doesn't make me any less a woman."

She waited. "Will you?"

I didn't respond right away. I thought the one person David was most smitten by was himself. Drunk with the chants of the crowd.

Or was I just being jealous, upset that the good-looking hero favored Michal with his attention while ignoring me?

"Don't help me," she finally said, bitterness in her voice. "Forget I asked. You're as evil as you pretend to be."

"Oh, stop," I said and agreed to help her.

I GOT MY CHANCE SOONER THAN I EXPECTED.

Father summoned me to his side in one of his chambers. We sat at a table and Father dismissed his guards, telling them to wait outside. He drank deeply from a cup and sighed. Mother sat beside him, looking pleased.

He got right to the point. "It is time that you be wed," he said. "You have become a woman and it is right that, as God provided Adam and Eve for each other, you should have a mate."

If Michal had made reference to Adam and Even during one of her endless discussions about true love, I'd have asked how well that one had worked out. But that didn't seem to be the right thing to say now.

I wanted to beg for more time. A year. Two years. Ten years. A lifetime. I wasn't ready for a man. I doubted that I'd ever be ready.

But I said, "Yes, Father."

He nodded. "Adriel, the son of Barzillai the Meholathite, has offered a dowry fitting for a king's daughter."

Father ran through a list of all of the man's virtues, chiefly being that he was rich enough to afford my dowry, but I barely listened.

Why couldn't I be like Michal, enthused about marriage? Most girls were like her. Or at least they were more accepting of the prospect than I was.

I cringed at the thought of a foul-smelling brute climbing atop me and inserting something repulsive into my most private place, all so I could get a baby inside me. A baby that would then hurt so much coming out that, by comparison, I wouldn't think the act that got it there in the first place was so awful.

Maybe I talked to the servant girls too much. Or to the wrong ones. Still, I didn't understand why anyone would look forward to that.

But I knew my place, so when Father finished, I said, "It would please me greatly to marry the man you have chosen. I hope that God will bless me with many male children."

Father and Mother nodded and smiled.

I felt like running from the room, but remembered my promise so I asked, "When will Michal marry? She, too, is a woman now."

They both were taken aback.

"After your marriage," Father said. "You are the eldest. Why do you ask?"

"Have you considered joining our house to David, son of Jesse?"

Father's face clouded over. He gripped the sides of his chair so tightly, his hands shook. "Must I hear his name from you too? Will even my own household speak of him?"

His eyes blazed and he began to shout. "Have you heard the chants when we return from battle? 'Saul has killed his thousands. David has killed his ten thousands.' What else is left for him? To take away my kingdom?"

I bowed my head, hoping that the madness would not overtake him. "Father, I meant no harm. Forgive my tongue for I speak when I should be quiet." I took a chance. "Though not as often as Michal."

He glared at me for a time, his face red, but then burst into laughter. "Not as often as Michal." He roared. "Of that you are right. That girl is never quiet."

I took one more chance. "Father, you are the king, the first one given by God to Israel. You need fear no poor shepherd's son. But if David's popularity becomes a danger, marry him to one of your daughters. Then he becomes an ally."

Father stared in wonderment. Mother looked on with confused fear, her gaze moving back between Father and me.

"He is but the youngest son of a poor shepherd," Father said. "How could he pay a dowry fitting a king's daughter?"

I drew in a deep breath. "Is not an ally worth more than any dowry a richer man could pay?"

Silence filled the room for a long time.

Then Father nodded, a smile forming upon his lips. "You have wisdom greater than all my advisors." He glanced at Mother and said, "So it shall be."

MICHAL SHRIEKED WITH DELIGHT AND HUGGED ME, BEGGING forgiveness for all the times she'd called me evil. Over and over, she pried me for details I might have forgotten.

Days later, we were summoned before the throne. We wore jewels and our finest tunics, covering our heads even though that wasn't required until the actual wedding ceremony.

As the eldest, I went first while Michal remained in a rear

antechamber. Mother and I stood behind Father's throne as the guards stepped outside. Flowers adored the walls. A musician played the lute and sang. I awaited Adriel the Meholathite.

In walked David.

I froze. What was he doing here? I glanced at Mother. She beamed.

When the lute player finished, Father began. "David, son of Jesse, you have become the greatest warrior in the kingdom," he said. "I have summoned you today to repay you. I offer my daughter's hand in marriage. Merab will make you a good wife and bear you many male children. I require only that you be valiant for me and fight the Lord's battles."

David's ruddy complexion turned pale. He looked to me. I averted my eyes. Michal would be furious. David didn't look too happy about it either.

"Oh, great king," he finally said. "Who am I? I am the least of all men, the youngest son of a poor shepherd from the least of the tribes. Who am I to be a son-in-law to the king?"

Heavy silence fell over the court.

He had rejected me? I wanted none of this man. I wanted none of any man. But to be offered to a poor shepherd and then scorned made me want to cover my head in shame. I had never felt such humiliation. I might not be pleasing to the eye, but I was the king's daughter.

"But…the people love you," Father said. "You are not the least of all men." Appearing unable to comprehend David's rejection, Father said, "I require no dowry but that you serve me in battle."

David bowed his head. "It is a great and kind offer, O King, but I cannot accept. Please offer Merab's hand to a man more worthy than I."

More worthy? His vanity knew no bounds, his chest swelling with pride when the people chanted of the king killing his thousands and David his ten thousands. He claimed not to be worthy?

I knew who he considered unworthy. Me!

Not that I wanted him, but had ever there been a king's daughter offered with no dowry but loyalty? That would be shame enough. But for such a woman to be considered so repugnant that even such an offer was refused was beyond the pale.

I ran from all these witnesses to my shame, and burst into the antechamber where Michal waited, almost knocking her over.

Mother followed behind. Her face ashen, she said, "Michal, go to your father. He awaits you."

Startled and confused, she left.

I buried my face in my hands. This was the problem with heroes. They became so filled with pride that even the lowliest of them—a poor shepherd!—could reject the hand of a king's daughter.

———

MICHAL FLEW BACK INTO THE ROOM IN A COLD RAGE. "You said you talked to Father!"

"I did, but he—"

"You stole David away from me! You don't love him. You only speak of him with scorn. How could you have done this?"

"I spoke for you, Michal, but Father heard what he wanted to hear."

"But—"

"Michal!" I said. "David rejected me."

She blinked. "Neither of us is getting married?"

I nodded.

"Because of the dowry?"

In a voice barely above a whisper, I said, "There was no dowry. David had to only pledge his loyalty."

Michal's eyes widened and for a time she said no more. Finally, she asked, "Do you think…he loves me?"

———

SO I MARRIED ADRIEL THE MEHOLATHITE.

Marriage hasn't been as bad as I imagined. Only on the six days leading up to the Sabbath do I pray that the Lord God strike me dead.

Father offered Michal's hand to David, though this time

with a dowry to be earned on the battlefield. With me out of the way, David no longer felt unworthy of being the king's son-in-law.

What a surprise.

I still believe that David's vanity will one day cause Michal pain as it does for so many who love heroes, but I've come to believe that he loves her too.

Perhaps it is one of those lies we tell ourselves often enough until we believe it—like David's killing of the lion and bear with his own hands—but I now accept that David's refusal was not a rejection of me but rather that he loved Michal and could accept no other.

That I can forgive.

For I cannot question his devotion.

You know a man is in love when he pays a dowry of two hundred Philistine foreskins.

POKER BOY

Read all his adventures at

wmgbooks.com

SCOTT EDELMAN

Long-time professional writer and editor Scott Edelman returns to these pages with a story with a bleak title, to say the least. But a story really worth reading.

Scott was the editor of the science fiction magazine Science Fiction Age. *He published and edited the semi-professional magazine* Last Wave *from 1982 to 1985. Other magazines edited by Edelman over the years include* Sci-Fi Universe, Sci-Fi Flix, *and* Satellite Orbit. *He became the editor of* SCI FI Magazine (*the official print magazine of* The Sci Fi Channel) *in 2002, and has edited the channel's online magazine* Science Fiction Weekly *since 2000.*

But he did write some for the early years of Pulphouse, (*yes, he has been around as long as I have*) *and now, his sixth story in this new incarnation is pure Edelman.*

For more information about Scott's writing and editing, go to www.scottedelman.com

THE FUTURE WILL BE WORSE

SCOTT EDELMAN

Joey, head down, shoulders hunched, eyes locked on the pavement directly in front of his feet, fumed about his future.

And not just his future—but the future.

He knew there were others—such as Cynthia, who a few moments before had slammed the door behind him after their latest (or maybe their last) argument—who dreamed of visiting that uncharted shore. But not him.

He'd never longed, as some did, of drowsing like Rip Van Winkle only to wake a lifetime later, or of building a time machine which would allow such a visit in a more scientific manner. He did not wonder what he would see in subsequent centuries if only it were possible to visit the distant times which lay in wait beyond his own years. No. Wonder—in any of its meanings—wasn't a word which could be used to describe his mind when he considered the future. Repulsion, maybe. Fear, perhaps. But never wonder.

As far as Joey was concerned—the future could go to Hell. He didn't want to end up there. Not even by traveling the simple way we all journey in that direction, one slow second at a time. Why would he, when he didn't even like the idea of the future?

All of which meant he from time to time found himself looking forward to the end of it all. Oh, it wasn't that he was suicidal. He simply didn't envy those who would live on to learn what would happen next. Since he couldn't put a brake on progress—or "progress," as he always thought of it—he didn't see the point.

He could sense tomorrow rushing toward him much too quickly, and though he did everything he could think of to avoid its swift approach, he knew his struggle was useless. The future was coming, and he had no say in the matter. Which meant the only outcome he could imagine for himself was to end up a sad old man who'd get himself drunk in bars to work up the nerve for singing a bad karaoke version of "My Way."

And in that vision, no one would ever clap, not even in pity.

But don't mistake the fact Joey feared the future to mean he was any kind of fan of the present. No, he didn't think life would be perfect if only he could lock that present in place. Because one of the reasons he didn't like tomorrow is because he didn't much like today either—since after all, today was nothing more than yesterday's tomorrow. It was that current tomorrow—the one which most days was already too much to bear, the one whose weight threatened to crush him most every moment—which had him tramping along the pavement with his hands bunched into fists stuffed deep into his jacket pockets.

And he suspected the next tomorrow—the true tomorrow —would only be worse.

For he didn't like the Internet (even though he barely remembered the time before it had arrived), or those who shaved body parts which weren't (according to him) intended to be shaved, or conversely, those who failed to shave those parts which were, or the proliferation of tattoos (which messed with what, to him, tattoos were meant to telegraph), or movies based on comic books.

He didn't like books based on comic books either.

Or women with short hair, men with long hair, men with earrings, women with nose rings, cable TV, textbooks with any facts beyond those which had been settled before he was born (and he would be happy to tell you which facts those were, though you wouldn't be at all happy by the time he was done, and even long before), pronouns (or what he thought were pronouns even as he used them all the time), foods spicier than those his mother had dared to make, or….

The list was endless. Or could be if circumstances were ever to need it to be.

He had no idea why he was that way. He didn't even know if he really wanted to be that way. He certainly didn't remember having chosen it. All he knew was that he was that way, regardless of how he'd gotten there, even though it often felt as if he were trapped in a too-tight sweater he couldn't get out of because the zipper was stuck. And so he'd grown to accept his lack of acceptance.

Another aspect of acceptance was—once all his grievances

were added up—he didn't accept you. Or your opinions. Or your friends. Or their opinions. Or, in fact, anybody's opinions but his own.

All of this came together to create the reason why—though Joey would deny it—Cynthia had shut that door on him.

Joey's potentially infinite list was also why he kept his head down as he moved quickly along. The less he saw of the new world coming into being—the fewer hints of tomorrow he spotted in the storefronts he walked by, or in the faces of those who walked by him—the more he believed he had a chance of dodging it. Which is why he stumbled with full force into a man walking toward him.

Joey didn't even realize what had happened until he'd bounced back and had already fallen to the pavement. He was about to complain loudly—he loved to complain—but something about the man—backlit by the sun, causing Joey to throw an arm up to block the glare—stopped him. In that moment, Joey was off balance more than literally, for he was confused and unable to understand—

Why, though he had been in motion, had the man not been knocked over, and he been the one to fall?

Maybe it's because he'd always been the one to fall.

"You don't want to go that way," the man said before Joey could splutter, or even begin to get to his feet. The sun made him seem to glow as he gestured with a thumb back over one shoulder toward where Joey had—without true intention, his direction being driven by a mix of anger and adrenaline, rather than any conscious choice—been heading. "That way is Thursday. Tuesday is back over there."

The man pointed to the other side of the street, and wriggled his palm like a fish—which cast a shadow across Joey's face, allowing him to drop his arm—to indicate he should head right once he returned back to the corner he'd passed without even noticing.

"I don't think time works that way," said Joey, settling into his ornery self again, which the shock of the collision had only temporarily subdued. "Don't you realize how ridiculous you sound?"

"Have it your way then," said the man. He stepped over Jocy, walked to that same intersection, then turned left, the opposite of what he'd indicated. Joey, feeling challenged, disrespected—and uncertain which of those insults angered him more—leapt to his feet and rushed after the man. Yet even though he reached the recommended street only a few steps after the stranger...the man was gone.

Joey stood in stasis, looking in turn down the way the man had disappeared, then the way he'd suggested Joey should go, then back again. What was he to do with such advice? What had been offered wasn't even information—it was delusion. Still, he stepped out into the crosswalk and paused between the two stretches of pavement—between the promised past and the inescapable future—considering which way he truly wanted to head.

He knew he'd been walking aimlessly since storming off— or being pushed out—from Cynthia, who'd insisted they needed time apart. (But when did time ever solve anything?) Replaying their last conversation left no room for anything else, so he'd never consciously picked a path, instead letting the path pick him. Perhaps it was time he chose which way to go, rather than—just—going.

So he turned his back on Thursday and walked toward where Tuesday could purportedly be found, staring for the first time that day not at the pavement, but in the direction of whatever waited ahead...which at first did little more than give him something new to grumble about.

For the streets didn't seem that much different than those he'd walk down on any ordinary day. The storefronts were all unfortunately still transformed into what he'd been forced to grow used to by the passing years. Tacquerias. Unisex barber shops. Vape shops. Cut-rate computer repair stores. He was disappointed in them for existing, and disappointed in himself for believing, even for an instant, this stroll might cause them not to be. But the stranger's promise was so aligned with his desires, how could he not believe, some-where deep where foolish hope resided? But he walked on anyway, for where else did he have to go? Certainly not the place he'd thought of as home. The locks there had likely already been changed.

But then, as he began to cross a street, he noticed (to his surprise) he had no difficulty in doing so, for the cars paused as soon as he entered the crosswalk. No one waved a middle finger, or shouted at him for blocking their way. And those on foot, when he arrived at the next stretch of pavement, seemed...different. They walked more slowly, almost ambling. The women's clothing was brighter, the men's duller. There were more visible smiles, and fewer visible piercings. Gone were the storefronts he loathed, replaced by shoe stores, a tobacconist, and...was that a barber pole he'd just walked past? It had been a long time since he'd seen one of those.

He'd only been at it for a few blocks—at least he'd thought it had only been a few blocks—but it was obvious he'd gone further back than—what was it that had been promised? Tuesday.

The thought caused him to speed up his steps.

As he reached the midpoint between one crossing and the next, the air smelled cleaner for a brief moment, as he balanced equidistant between the smell of engines and the smell of beasts. He would have liked to pause there in the untarnished air, but feared he would lose what lay ahead— behind?—if he lingered.

The next street was even easier to cross than those just past. No cars needed to pause their hurry to let him through, for there were no cars. Only horses crisscrossed his path now, bearing men, pulling carriages. He slipped past them easily.

THEN HE NOTICED THOSE WHO NOW WALKED TOWARD HIM ONCE he reached the other side did not smile. Frowning, they split as they saw him coming, picking up speed to better keep clear. But he didn't care that they winced at whatever whiff of the future remained on him. He never cared what others thought of him—a necessary contradiction for someone who cared so deeply about what others thought—and saw no reason to start now. He only cared for what they appeared to be willingly leaving behind. He knew that precious past waited for him off in the distance.

The streets beside him, which had begun asphalt, then briefly changed to cobblestone, had now become mud. Others might see that as a defect, but not Joey, for to him, that was the way they were meant to be. He'd from time to time tried to explain that to Cynthia, but never with the right words. He wished she could be with him, walking away from what was wrong with the world.

He walked so long he grew tired, odd since the distance he'd covered seemed to have only been measured in blocks, so his weariness made little sense, but he thought he might sit on the curb anyway. There was no curb, though, not as he remembered them, for there was no longer even a true side-walk. The concrete which had once been under his feet had been replaced by wooden boards, and he hadn't noticed when he'd left that part of his past behind. He plopped down on the walkway and let his feet dangle into the dirt. He considered how far he'd come, and how far he had still to go.

He could see the street continuing on, with the sparse buildings on either side no longer tall and of brick and steel, but instead low and wooden and with blank spaces between.

The world was growing younger, though to see the missing pieces had him thinking of an old man who'd lost many of his teeth. Rather than continuing on in that direction, he thought perhaps he'd stop right there—for all which had annoyed him seemed long gone, back somewhere behind him along the street which he'd come. It seemed wrong to waste the opportunity he'd been given, though, so he put the future to his back and continued walking on toward his past.

Further buildings fell away behind him, and when the last one vanished, and he was no longer hemmed in by humanity, he found he didn't care. So he walked on until the streets themselves were no more, and had become a path worn through the tall grass by those who'd gone before.

And then not even a path at all, but merely grass which had been beaten down.

And then not even that.

There suddenly seemed no way forward or back, not a clue to show anyone had ever stepped onto that spot or moved on from it, almost as if he'd been dropped from the air into a primeval field which had never known a human. He peered into the distance, but there were no landmarks with which to orient himself, and he sensed no matter how long he waited, the sun would never set and no stars would appear in the sky to guide him. He pushed forward anyway, hoping that even though there was no way to be sure, he was hewing to a straight line.

He stepped heavily on the grass, pushing it down firmly under his heels, figuring he could then use the new path carved behind him to orient himself to the direction he needed to walk ahead so he would not unwittingly circle back. But each time he turned, he found the field behind unblemished.

Yet he kept walking.

The ground beneath his feet eventually felt softer, then damp, and ultimately squishy. A foot sank in up to his ankle, and when he pulled back, his sock soaked and muddy, he saw he'd left a shoe behind. He plunged a hand beneath the surface, but the shoe sank away before he could retrieve it. No matter. He kicked off the other so he'd keep his balance as he went on. He thought of that shoe store behind him, and how many blocks, how many years, were between them, and did not care.

He continued on as the grass around him thinned, then faded, and found himself before a body of water so vast he couldn't tell whether it was lake or ocean, the other side too far to see. He looked both ways along the line where land and water met, uncertain where to wander next. Off to his left, he could see in the distance that land begin a gentle rise into a cliff, though through the mist which came off the water, he had no idea how high it rose. But he would find out.

He headed that way, toes squelching and slipping inside his socks, until in exasperation he kicked them away. He regretted, when the mud gave way to rock, that he'd tossed away that second shoe, but it was too late for him to do anything but walk on barefoot.

The rock rose, and he rose with it, until the shoreline was no more and he stood on a cliff face. Laid out before him in one direction, beginning a measureless distance below, the water which seemed to know no end, while in the other, as the land sloped down to sea level, he could make out the string of progress—"progress"—which led back to the future from which he'd come. He could see the entire history of the world in a single vista—the water from which all life crawled, the first shelters other than caves, which were barely more than branches leaning against each other, the mud huts melting in the rain, the wooden shacks which grew into houses, their occupants surely having the feeling the species had gone as far as it could go, followed by skyscrapers and malls and all the ingredients of the world from which he'd fled. The megalopolis beyond which he could not see seemed impossibly far away, and yet—he'd only just walked from there...hadn't he? And it had only taken him a few hours...hadn't it?

"You weren't supposed to have come this far," said someone so close by Joey's side he could feel the speaker's breath on the back of his neck.

He jerked away, and as he stepped back, almost fell into the sea. He turned to see the man who'd pointed him toward the patch of land on which he stood just...this morning? His back was to Joey now, his shoulders hunched.

"You're not supposed to be here," he added, his voice low and sad. "It's time you went back. The yesterday you long for isn't here—it's still in the future."

Joey turned away from the man who suddenly seemed too sad to contemplate, so he could instead stare off to where his journey had begun.

"The future isn't what it's cracked up—"

———

"—TO BE," SAID JOEY, STARTLED TO FIND HIMSELF ON HIS BACK on the pavement, looking up once again at the man whom he'd bounced off, the man who once more crowned with a halo by the sun looked down at him, the man who'd told him how to get to the mountaintop, and then, once he arrived there, appeared yet again only to cast him away.

No, not cast him away. Push him away.

Contradictory memories merged in his mind to show the way to his current moment—of falling from an impossibly high cliff to land there, of colliding on a city street to stumble there—but which had been real or whether both had been real did not matter, for here he was, back where his journey to Tuesday had begun. This time, though, the man, who seemed at first about to speak, just as he had before, did not. Instead, he stepped over him, walked to the corner, and turned so quickly Joey could not rise in time to see which way he had gone.

Joey leapt up, winced when his bare feet touched the hot pavement, and—gingerly—raced to the corner. But the stranger was once again gone. And yet, even though this time, no words had been spoken, no directions given, he knew what he had to do.

He attempted to cross the street so he could again head to the past, and perhaps this time not overshoot his intended destination, whenever that was meant to be—for maybe that's what had gone wrong—right?—only now, no cars would stop for him. No matter how he studied the traffic, no break appeared into which he could insert himself. He occasionally took a step forward, hoping to catch the eyes of a driver, cause them to hit the brake, but always had to fall back.

He got the message.

He did not like the message—he rarely did—but he understood. So he turned away from the path to yesterday, and instead continued on the way he'd previously been heading, even though he knew, as he always knew, the future would undoubtedly be worse.

His earlier wandering had begun almost unconsciously, meaning the initial changes to the world perceived during that first journey had come without him necessarily noticing them, his awareness arising only when they'd grown so numerous as to be impossible to ignore. But this time, he walked with intent, paying careful attention to each passing step as today slipped away.

Once he'd turned, nothing impeded his passage. Cars no longer interfered with his ability to cross each intersection, for what vehicles there were—wheel-less, bubble-domed, and with broad fins which seemed to serve no purpose—floated above the pavement. There was no need to pause at each corner because they floated by just above his head, not even ruffling his hair with their passing. Oddly, not only did none of the cars seemed old, but neither did any of the people. Everyone who walked, everything that whizzed by, seemed bright and shiny—life which to him showed no signs of life.

The vape shops and other annoying establishments faded to be replaced by storefronts offering oxygen in a variety of flavors, several of which he did not recognize, and through one window he could see baristas handing out, not multi-hyphenate coffees, but patches which customers reached back to slap against the napes of their necks. He couldn't imagine what those latter purchases promised, and had no interest in pausing his forward march so he could find out.

Soon those who meandered beside him stopped walking, but they did not stop moving, instead hovering along in their chosen direction without needing to shuffle their feet. The space between their shoes and the pavement was infinitesimal, but it was enough. Though it wasn't the shoes themselves which propelled them so effortlessly, for sometimes the feet of those so elevated were bare. And sometimes

...WHAT WAS BARE WAS MORE THAN JUST THEIR FEET. WHATEVER fashion was to come was apparently as exasperating as what he'd left behind, and he wanted no part of it. Though even as he grumbled, he had to admit he was glad his own hovering meant he no longer had to scrape his bare feet against hot concrete.

However ridiculous those around him appeared—sometimes wearing their garments and sometimes trailed by them, with straps and sparkles and bangles and belts and even a miasma of mist in colors he never knew existed—the people —if people they still were—seemed happy with it. All of them, every single one, even those still wearing glasses, or walking with a cane, or rolling along in a chair. The only time that happiness fled their faces was when they looked at him, which was, he knew, the way he'd looked at the rest of the world before this all had begun. Luckily, they behaved the same as he had, and looked only, their discomfited expressions offering an occasional sneer. He wondered what they saw when they perceived and avoided him. But he did not have time to wonder long, for soon it was not merely the people alone who were in motion, but the streets themselves.

The pavement beneath his feet now moved him forward— without him ever noticing when it had begun—faster than he could move himself. And soon, that wasn't the only thing moving, for the storefronts themselves rose and flew about, dancing into different configurations as they launched off to better meet customers, who had also taken to the sky, creating an array so dizzying he dropped his head as he once had, back before a stranger had sent him wandering. Only this time, it was not merely to ignore an unsatisfying world, but to hit pause on the vertigo the swirling vision had brought on.

He did not look up again until he reached the unexpected end of the speeding walkway and was hurled into a bed of ash. The sky was filled with smoke, and when he turned, he could no longer see what lay behind through the dark clouds which curtained the past. He found he did not mourn the loss of yesterday, for he knew that what he needed no longer waited there. All that lay ahead, though, was further ash—ash, ash, ash, as far as he could see—which did not seem a pleasant future at all. He was not disconcerted, for it confirmed everything he expected about the future.

He trudged forward, dragging his feet through all that remained, sending up puffs of dust behind him, hoping he continued to walk in a straight line along the path which had, he felt, been promised. He wondered how long the ash could go on, for there seemed to be no end to it. And then, suddenly, as if each step had carried him miles, he did arrive at the ash's end.

He arrived at water.

He did not have to wonder long what kind of water, whether lake or ocean, for across the expanse of blue, he spotted a familiar cliff, one on which he had not so long ago— or maybe it had been thousands of years—stood. He was no longer sure how to count time, or whether time even still counted at all.

He stepped forward until his toes touched the water, which felt cool on one foot, warm on the other, a fact which might have unsettled him once, but he was beyond being unsettled. The cliff which he had climbed, the cliff from which he'd fallen, didn't seem that far away, and since he considered himself a pretty decent swimmer, and the water was calm, he thought he could make it there. If he did, he'd have completed a circuit, which felt like the right to do so. Maybe it was the only thing he could do.

As he unbuckled his belt, a voice once more came from beside and behind him, the speaker once again much too close, and this time, he did not jerk away.

"You again," said the stranger who had started it all.

When Joey turned to look at the man, he was no longer standing, lips to his ear, but kneeling below him with his fingers stroking the skin of the water.

"I told you," he continued. "You're not supposed to be here. You haven't understood a single thing I've said."

"So if not here, then where am I supposed to be?"

"That's for you to discover, but definitely not here. I offered you a gift—and you wasted it."

And with that, he swept a hand into the back of Joey's knees, knocking him into the water. Submerged in the shallows which were suddenly deep, he coughed and choked and kicked his way to the surface, only to discover he hadn't actually risen atop water at all, but was yet again on the pavement where all this had begun, Cynthia's slamming of their door still a recent wound. Though he was on his back, the man who'd sent him there—the man who kept sending him there—was nowhere to be seen.

He clambered to his feet, spitting out water which his present circumstances told him had no reason to be. He had no idea whether to go forward or back, or whether he would be free to go either of those ways even if he could make up his mind.

He thought of Cynthia, with whom it seemed he had no future, Cynthia, with whom he had no trouble making up his mind, Cynthia, with whom, now that he thought about it, he hardly had a past. The future, as he had found out, just as he'd expected, would be worse, the past had ejected him—

But what about the present?

He studied the row of storefronts on the street where his day had truly started, his senses assaulted one after the other by everything he hated—a coffee shop serving more than two kinds of coffee, a vape shop offering a substitute experience which could never replace the reality of tobacco, a beauty parlor promising it also did waxing for men, a tattoo parlor willing to make permanent and visible what should be kept to one's own damn self, then forgotten, plus numerous other offensive establishments stretching from corner to corner.

One after another, he patronized them all.

AND ONCE HE WAS DONE AND BACK OUT ON THE SIDEWALK, A macchiato in his left hand and a vape pen in his right, a stud through his left ear and a tattoo of the cliff on which he'd stood etched on his right shoulder, with his skin of his body as smooth as a newborn baby's and a haircut he was sure made him look like a buffoon—only then did he know he was ready to go back again. Not a lot this time, not all the way to the beginning of things, but a little.

Time to go back to Cynthia.

He was ready. He would show her he could change. One look and she would know.

When he arrived back at what had once been his front door, the coffee cup was empty and the vape pen no longer functioning. (He hadn't actually paid that much attention to the instructions. After all, did cigarettes need instructions? Life didn't used to require instructions.) He kept his grip on them both anyway, though. He needed her to see them. He needed her to see it all. Only after he'd rolled up his right sleeve to make sure the tattoo was visible did he knock. He could have tried his key, but didn't want to find out she'd gone ahead and so quickly changed the locks as she'd threatened before the slamming of the door.

Though...hadn't he stormed off from that spot only a few minutes ago? He couldn't be sure. The space between his leaving and his return seemed at once both an instant and forever. She likely wouldn't have had the time. Even so...he sensed entering unbidden wouldn't have been the best idea. Because that's what the old Joey would have done, and he needed to make sure Cynthia could see there was a new Joey.

He stopped breathing as the door began to open, and

when she came into view, and her eyes widened as she saw him, he hoped the many changes to his appearance, combined with his (hopefully) contrite expression (he'd tried as best as he could to don one) had begun the conversation for him before he even started speaking. Which he made sure he did before she could.

"You were wrong about me, Cynthia," he said. He thought, even as he said the words, that surely she could see that without him having to say them. "See? I can change. I can. Things don't have to be the way they were. I don't have to be the way I was. How about we give this thing another chance?"

She was his past and future. He knew that. How could she not?

She didn't answer immediately, which he allowed himself to accept as a good sign, because whenever she did come back with a quick answer, whatever happened next wasn't going to go well for him. Then, instead of responding with words, she sighed, followed by the action which was her true answer—the slow closing of the door, which stabbed at his heart more deeply than her previous slamming of it.

When the deadbolt slid into place, he thought he'd never heard anything that loud. The sound surprised him so—how could she not understand what all the changes he'd been through had wrought?—he dropped his sagging cup and vape pipe both. He stood there in its echo waiting for the sound of the lock snapping open again, for surely she would regret the finality of her action—and when it did not come, after a sigh of his own, he removed the ear stud he'd hoped would help persuade her and dropped it beside the two objects which had already slipped from his hands.

Let them be his final gifts to her.

Fingers bloody, he staggered away from their door—now her door—wondering...why then had he been put through such a day? A day during which he'd wandered millennia expecting they would lead him back to her? She needed time apart, she'd said, and he'd given her time, hasn't he? All of time. Then looped around to where he'd begun to find nothing had changed except the superficial. And now he was trapped in that loop, one from which there didn't seem to be any way out.

But perhaps there was one—for it suddenly occurred to him as he stepped a second time that same day from his door —or what had once been his door—that if he walked down the right street, at the right time, at the right speed, he could perhaps catch up with himself—time would allow that, wouldn't it?—to tell himself where he really needed to go, what he truly needed to do.

And as that triumphal thought came to him of how he could break free, it was superseded by a sudden memory which brought on a sickly feeling. He froze in place, blinded to his surroundings, and the moment he did so, staggered slightly as something bounced off him.

Not just something.

Someone.

Someone heedlessly rushing somewhere had slammed into him and now lay on his back on the pavement.

Joey looked down in horror into the face of the past, into his own face, and knew that, yes, just as he'd always suspected —the future would be worse.

And there wasn't anything he could do about it.

NINA KIRIKI HOFFMAN

Acclaimed veteran fantasy writer Nina Kiriki Hoffman is known for writing fantastically fun fantasy, and some amazingly dark stories that will twist you up. This is one sort of walks the line, a wonderful fantasy with a darkness running through it.

Nina is a musician, a writing instructor, and a judge for Writers of the Future.

And she is also amazingly fun to be around if you get the chance.

IMMERSED IN MATTER

NINA KIRIKI HOFFMAN

I admit it, after fifteen years of denying it: I, Owl out of Ginger, am half human, more my father's son than ever I thought.

Everyone in my generation of faery has a human half. We all have the same human father. We never speak of it.

The race of faery was dying until our father came, sent as an ensorcelled emissary by our dead king. Before he came, the only new children to enter the underground lands in three hundred years were those born of human women, half-bloods, never as gifted as their faery fathers. Most halfbloods stayed aboveground among humans, where their pieces of gifts could serve them well; the few who came to our lands were treated as lesser beings, servants or sometimes slaves.

The faery I knew my own age or near it were my half-brothers and sisters. What fraction of our human father was in us was too small to show. Each of us was beautiful and skilled. We seemed entirely faery to everyone, with no stink or stamp of human on us. Most of us resembled our mothers, so we all looked different from each other, and our gifts were as strong as any among the purebloods. We were gifted with acceptance as the next generation of faery.

Like everyone else, I never looked twice at the halfbloods who had been born aboveground, except to notice they were different, lesser. They smelled strange. Fit for kitchen work, laundry work, work that involved dirt. Fit to pass among us as shadows.

My mother sang over my cradle when I was little about what kind of creature my father had been. She had loved him. She remembered him. She wished he would return.

I took it for a human tale and believed it not, just something with which to scare children. None of the other children I played with had mothers who sang these kinds of songs.

My generation was taught as previous generations had been, left to find our own interests and then pursue them as our gifts developed, finding our own teachers. Mother taught me the basics of magic and survival, but my favorite teacher was Golden, who knew the languages and shapes of animals.

My mother was not happy with my choice of specialties—shapeshifters acknowledged our kinship with lesser beings, and so they were disdained by the snottiest among us—but she indulged me, since that was where my gift lay.

Golden and I went up the tunnels and through the gates into the world above, where the lights in the sky changed and so did the temperature of the air, and water came falling out of the sky as well, not just flowing in streams and lakes and springs. We wandered wild lands, swamps and forests, meeting animal people and seeing what they could be persuaded to do. Golden had a gift for speaking with wolves and foxes. Bird language came more swiftly to my tongue. Golden taught me many lesser dialects, and together we learned cat language, though cats great and small ignored us when they liked, whether we got the accents right or not.

My greatest dream was to talk with horses.

I wanted to be a horse or own a horse. They related to people in a different way than other animals. They were so large and powerful, and yet they suffered humans to use them and ride them. I wanted to meet, know, and ride a horse. I wanted to discover the reasons for their cooperation with something they could trample.

Unfortunately, most horses lived with humans. Golden said horses ran wild halfway around the world, in places with lots of sand, but there was no gate that opened from our underground to that part of the world.

By choice, Golden would have kept me in the wilderlands always, but because I was fascinated by horses, I spent much of my aboveground time lurking near a road that led through the forest to a city. Traffic was frequent. Horses pulled carts of fruit, flour, and vegetables from the surrounding country to the city markets. Mounted messengers and soldiers traveled along the road. Travelers in caravans rode horses or drove them, and guards traveled with them, on horseback. Traders and tinkers went both ways in horse-drawn wagons.

Some of the horses that pulled the carts were massive and slow, some smaller and sturdy. Those that carried the messengers were quick and alert, and those I liked best of all.

I listened to everything, to the little herd dogs as they ran and nipped the flanks of goats and sheep, to the cud-chewers and the tinkers' cats, but most of all I listened for words from the horses. I only half-understood their tales of travel and grass and water, fighting and running and carrying people. Their voices were low and wonderful.

Golden disapproved of my desire to know horses, so I had to sneak off to study them when he set me other tasks. Most often I went to the Feather Inn, a day's ride from the city, and watched the human boys who worked in the stables. They saddled and unsaddled horses, removed, repaired, replaced bits and reins, combed and brushed the animals, fed and watered them and picked rocks and muck out of their hooves. They spread straw on the ground when it was too muddy, and mucked out the stalls, and slept above the horses in the hay.

At first I could not stand the stench of humans, but eventually I became accustomed.

ONE FROSTY EVENING AT THE LEADING EDGE OF WINTER, WHEN Golden had sent me out to study the night habits of deer, I crouched under a bush with one of the inn yard cats. She was pregnant and hungry. I had brought her a fresh-killed rat. I wanted to buy conversation with her.

"How can I get close enough to speak with horses?" I whispered.

"You won't be able to, not while you stink of faery," the cat said.

"What's wrong with how I smell?"

"We know your kind means us no good," said the cat. She had eaten the rat already and edged away from me as we spoke.

"I don't mean you any harm, or them either."

She flattened her ears. "All too often an incautious animal disappears though a faery gate and is never seen again."

I hugged my green-clad knees and thought about that. I had seen animals underground, cats, dogs, even a tribe of foxes in one slowtime pocket where my aunt lived. The queen had a stable with horses in it, but it was fenced around with spell protections so strong I could never get near it. Whenever I tried to approach, I found myself wandering the farthest reaches of the kingdom without any memory of how I had gotten there.

"I just want to talk to them. I don't want to steal them."

"I know the worth of a faery promise," she said.

Well, perhaps she was right. If I really wanted to speak with a horse, my best chance might be to find one of my own.

"Don't you think one of them would rather have me for a master?" I asked the cat. "Are humans so good to horses that horses want to stay with them always? Humans hit them with sticks and straps. Humans make them work even when they're too tired and old. Isn't there a single horse who would rather leave this place with me?"

"There might be," said the cat. "I don't generally speak with horses. They allow humans too much liberty. Get yourself inside and ask, but before you try, you'd better find a safer scent, or the cock will crow, the dogs will bark, and even the mice will squeak at you. Thanks for the rat." She slipped away.

A safer scent. A safer scent. I thought of the transforming lessons I'd had from Golden, who had taught me to change myself into an owl, my namesake. I could fly into the stables; perhaps none would be the wiser.

Golden had taught me two transformations: owl, and wolf. At this stage in my magecraft, I could only transform into things that were part of my heritage, animals in my bloodline, and those were the only two who had left clear enough tracks. Sometime deep in the well of our history there was a binding together with animals to acquire powers, and most of us shared some animal blood, though many tried to deny it, and many more never learned to work with it.

I melted back into the forest half a league, found a safe place up a tree, and called the owl out of me. The night shifted shape as I changed, became a place sounds and sights more intense, bright, and sharp. There was no solid darkness: I could see everywhere, and the sky was a place of many lights but no color. I spread silent wings and lofted, drifted through the air, scanned the ground beneath the trees for any sign of squeak. Transformation always made me hungry.

Two mice and one vole later, I returned to the inn. Did I still stink of faery? I couldn't tell. I sifted scents. My relationship to them had changed too: many things smelled much more enticing to me, and things I would like as my faery self disgusted me now. The stable appealed to me because it was home to mice and rats and possibly baby birds. I flew in through the open hayloft door, delighting in the rustles of mice in the straw, alert to the sounds and scents of human, horse, and jingling tack from the floor below. I found a perch on one of the beams where I could look past the hayloft down into the stables.

Below me, horses. Warm and huge and smelling of hay and sweat and their own less-than-leather wild scent, a scent of things that run. Did I have any horse in me? Until I could see how deep their language ran in me, I could not tell.

A hoot flowed out of me, my delight in being closer to horses than I ever had before.

Below me, some boy looked up. "An owl," he said.

"A death bird! Scare it away," said another.

Two boys climbed up into the loft and pulled rocks from their pockets. They stoned me. "Get out of our stable! Go prophesy death somewhere else!"

I flew away, stinging in several places where rocks had struck me. I found my tree again and roosted there to brood. An owl wasn't welcome, even if nothing knew it was faery. A wolf would be even more unwelcome. Dogs, the warped wolves who lived with humans, resented their wild cousins, and humans feared wolves. When I first learned wolf shape, I had sneaked up on humans camped in the forest and scared them from their fires, horses, and possessions.

Golden made me stop. He said such actions put other wolves at risk.

Horses hated wolves too. Even when I'd chased off their humans, horses at campsites wouldn't let me approach them.

I climbed back into my faery self, then dropped to the ground. I did a seek spell that took me to a place where deer were overnighting, and I spent the rest of the night watching them from a tree. Did my scent disturb them? It didn't. Toward morning I climbed down and approached them. None feared me enough to run from me or threaten me. The young one even let me touch it.

My sister-friend Henna was drawn to deer, though she couldn't take their shape. Her gifts lay in other directions: she could weave things into being.

I talked with these deer and couldn't understand why Henna liked them. So much of their orientation was fear, because they knew they were food to so many other things. Where was the fun in being something that ran away?

I went home at dawn, wondering why Golden made me

study animals like these. The answer to that turned out to be simple: he wanted me to study everything. He gave me raspberry tea with ambrosia in it, sweet, tart, and fortifying, and we sat by the green fire on his hearth, below bunches of drying aboveground herbs that hung from his ceiling. "You have time, Owl, ages and ages. You never know when something you learn today will serve you in the future. Just now we're living in peaceful times, but suppose there's a revolution or an invasion. It happens. If you know deer tactics as well as wolf and owl tactics…mole tactics, ant tactics, slug tactics. Learn everything."

After tea and questions I went home to my mother's house under the unweathering sky of the underground, where time does not divide into days so easily as above.

How was I going to get closer to horses? The animals that did: mice and rats. Chickens sometimes ran through the stables, but humans were too inclined to kill and roast them. Even if I could have turned into them—and I couldn't—I didn't want to be a prey animal.

I had tried to learn cat transformation, but as far as I could detect I didn't have that heritage either. Later in life, when I was older and had acquired knowledge, wisdom, and skills, perhaps I would be able to transform into animals whose heritage I didn't own, but that might take a hundred years, and I wanted horses now.

I lay on my feathersilk mattress, the scents of aboveground herbs around me—Golden gave me some to sleep on, for sharpening the brain, he said—and thought. What animal got closest to horses without being questioned?

Humans.

I had human in my heritage, though I'd spent my whole short life trying to forget or deny it. I owned human heritage with such a clear link that I could imagine the transformation without trouble, after all this time of trying to push it aside.

If I accepted it—

I curled tight on my mattress and hugged my spiderwoven blanket to my chest. I had looked away so long. I turned my eyes inward and saw the streak of self that had come from my father. It lay along my spine, cradled my bones. At first I thought it was gray, but when I really paid attention, I saw that it was shimmery and strange, all colors in turns. It looked like no human thing I had seen before.

I reached toward it, felt it engage me, then realized how tired I was after a night of running, spying, and observations. I banished the father self back to its hiding place and fell asleep.

GOLDEN AND I WENT ABOVEGROUND AGAIN WHEN NIGHT WAS falling there. "Tonight I want you to watch tree snakes," he said.

Ice had formed along the edges of the creek, crisped the surfaces of puddles, furred the dead leaves on the ground. I pulled my cloak tighter around me. Snakes? "But Teacher, they're hibernating now."

The first time I had seen snow aboveground, I had fallen in love with it, its whiteness, the way it packed into balls, and yielded and cushioned when I lay on it, the way it lay on everything and changed the look of the landscape, especially under the moon; I only noticed cold could hurt me later. Now I knew about frost and snow and ice: I knew to wear warm things and keep enough energy on tap to fire my blood when necessary.

"So?" Golden said. "Spend a quiet night watching them in their sleep. Note how they store and conserve their energy. Another tactic you may find useful later."

"I want to try something else tonight."

"Oh?" Golden hunched nearer me, eyes aglitter. He wore a pelt with heavy fur over his shoulders, the fur the same color as his tangled wealth of red-gold hair. I had wondered often whether it was the pelt of an animal self he had shed or if he had actually killed something to gain it. "Have you found another heritage animal?"

"I have."

"What is it?"

I raised a shoulder in case he wanted to clout me, and whispered, "Human."

For a long while he only stared, red fire in his eyes so they shone in the shadow that was his face. At last, he said, "Ah."

I waited, then lowered my shoulder when he didn't raise his fist.

He took my hand and led me far through the forest, away from the gate. When we reached one of his workspaces, a clearing with an underground chamber he had built where he stored baskets and the glass clippers he used when herb gathering, we stopped. It was a place only Golden and I knew. No one from underground would stumble over us here.

"I've been expecting this," he said in a voice that was more growl than faery.

"You have?"

"Only from you, Owl. Any of the others who've come to me for lessons would never take this step. I know you haunt the roadways and the inn yard."

"I want to speak with horses."

"As fine an excuse as any," he muttered.

"What?"

"Never mind. Have you opened to your heritage?"

"Not yet."

"Do it now, where I can supervise."

I lay on the dirt floor of his underground pocket and quieted my mind. I knew where to find the father self. I had only to glance at it, and it reached for me. Wait. "Golden," I said, "Did you ever meet my father?"

"I did."

"What was he like?"

"A difficult question, young Owl. He was never the same

twice. It depended on who looked at him and what she wanted. He came to my house once, when he was between
women, a state I never saw him in again. That was the only
time I saw him without a glamour on him. I gave him tea and
fruitbread."

"What was he like?" I asked again.

"He was very young," said Golden.

"Teacher. What was he like?"

Golden laughed. "There were many questions I wanted to
ask him. Who was he? Where did he come from? How did
the dead king choose him? This was before any of you had
been born, but three of you were coming. Those who longed
for children were not yet anxious about claiming their time
with him; there were no babies to see, envy, cherish, judge yet,
so he was untried except in those two ways, that he could
satisfy the ones he slept with, and quicken them. I never
found him free again."

"But what—"

"When I found him, he had just finished the time he spent
with Raven. I saw her hug him and kiss him good-bye and
leave him in the common room of the queen's palace. She
wove a black feather into his hair. For her, he had been dark
and tall and strong, with silver eyes. She touched his cheek
and left him, and he melted."

"Melted," I repeated.

"Melted into what he must have looked like before. A boy
not much older than you, with brown hair and hazel eyes,
handsome but not particularly interesting as humans can be
interesting. He looked — like many other humans. He
looked tired and sad. I took him home and gave him tea and

watched him. His hands shook until after he had some of my fruitbread. I had all my questions ready, and I never asked a single one."

I lay silent. Presently, Golden said, "Fireweed came to my house to find him. She sat at my table and watched him finish his tea. He thanked me, then turned to her and smiled and changed into a tall white-haired giant with a beard to his waist and shoulders broader than mine. Her eyes filled with longing and delight. She led him away. I didn't see him again for three months, and at that point, he was going off with Barley, and he had changed into a slender yellow-haired minstrel."

"What did he look like for my mother?"

Golden scratched his nose and studied me. "His hair was black and thick like yours, and his eyes were yellow, like yours."

My mother had peppery red hair and orange eyes. I was one of the few in my generation who didn't look like his mother. I had always wondered where my coloring came from, but had never let myself ask. No one treated me as though I looked like a human. In fact, I looked a bit like Otter, a friend of my mother's.

"I resemble my father's glamour?" That didn't make sense. A glamour was for appearance, not for seed.

"Those of you who don't look like your mothers look like what your mothers desired of your father."

I shook my head. I had never heard of magic like that.

"Open to your heritage, Owl."

Which heritage? What my father looked like, or who he had been? I closed my eyes and reached back to that pale many-colored place along my spine I knew came from my father.

I had thought it only a small fraction of myself, a part I could ignore, but as soon as I opened to it, it threaded all through me, a faint and gentle warmth that tendrilled out to my edges. I felt my organs squeeze and shift. My face tightened, and the bones of my skull closed in a little. The tips of my ears tingled, then shrank.

Too late, I thought, what if this change consumes me so I forget how to restore myself? My animal changes had been governed by the much stronger part of my heritage I had from my mother. Even though everything in my body changed, my largest self remained intact.

My father had given me at least half of myself. What if his half was strong enough to swallow what my mother had given me?

The final tingles and spirals of change faded from my soles and palms and stomach. I lay with my eyes shut, sensing myself.

The air felt colder on my face, and the scents of the night were fainter. Sounds had faded. At last I opened my eyes and found the night was dark, darker than I had ever seen it. I was surrounded by shadows, and I couldn't see through them well enough to know what cast them. "Golden?" I whispered. Breath frosted as it rose from my mouth. My voice tasted strange. I had lost the edge that let me say things and make them true.

"Here." He was a large looming shadow above me. He moved, opened his hands to let out yellow light.

I sat up and took stock of myself. I smelled my hand. Oh, yes. Though the scent was faint, it was human, not my own. My fingers were longer, but square-tipped instead of tapered, and I only had four fingers and a thumb now on each hand. My skin had darkened to a color of those who lived outside aboveground during the day: I had lost my underground pallor.

I touched my cheek, felt my nose. Bigger. My eyebrows felt heavier, but my hair was finer, and there was less of it. "What do I look like?" I asked. My tongue against the inside of my teeth felt different too.

Golden sketched a circle in the air. It filled with silver, an air mirror that showed me my new self.

I looked like half the stableboys at the inn, human and nondescript. I touched my hair: no longer black and thick, some shade of brown I couldn't see very well with these eyes, and my eyes were a darker color than they had been, wider and not so slanted.

After a moment, recognition flickered through me. Somewhere I had seen this self before. I closed my eyes and chased the fragment of memory. There was a taste in it: peach. I had sat in my mother's lap when she was much taller than I, and a man with this cleanshaven face sat close beside her, touching along arm and thigh. We were all on the big soft blue chair in my mother's bedroom, close enough that I could smell him. He smelled strange, different from everyone I'd met before, but I didn't think, then, that he smelled bad. He smiled down at me and gave me a slice of peach, ripe and sweet,which melted on my tongue and tasted of the above-ground season of summer and a sun I hadn't seen yet.

He kissed my forehead and stroked my hair, and my mother let him. He shared the peach with me and my mother until it was gone and we licked the last sweet, sticky juice off our fingers. We sat together like that for a long time, until someone else came and called him away. His eyes turned sad. He touched my hand and left.

"Oh, this is strange." I felt my face and frowned at the mirror.

Father. I had met him. I wore my father's face.

I turned from the mirror and looked at the night. Every direction I turned, I saw nothing but lighter darkness against dark, except when I looked up. The sky held stars, but they were smaller and dimmer than I remembered. "I feel so— weak. Blind and deaf and scent-deaf."

I struggled to my feet. I felt infant-weak and clumsy.

In the other transformations I knew, I had gained things as I lost other things. Owl gave me flight, and night sight so strong the world looked as well-lit as day, and hunting, and hearing so acute I could hear a mouse's footfall from the sky. Wolf had given me speed and scent appreciation and strength. What was good about this change? I was the same shape I had been, almost, but weaker in every aspect that I could measure.

Horses.

Father?

No. Now I could approach horses. That was the point. I shook my head, jarred loose the peach memory and let it sink away.

Why had I changed here, so far from the Feather Inn? It would take me ages to get there in this form.

The easy answer was to change into an owl or a wolf and fly or run, then change back to this when I was nearly there. I held out my right arm and thought, Wing.

Nothing happened.

"Golden," I whispered. Was I trapped for the rest of my life in this form? Had I doomed myself to a short hard life and an early death?

"Oh, dear," he said.

I hated my father!

"Wait," said Golden. "Open to your heritage, Owl."

As a human, I couldn't summon up the instant change I had managed as myself. But perhaps—

I lay down again and closed my eyes, looked inside myself. For a long while I saw nothing, just the dark I couldn't see through with the senses I had now. Then something sparked and shone. A glimmer along my spine, a heat under my skin. The more I studied it, the stronger it grew. I opened to it, felt it wash away what I was and restore me to what I had been.

I owned my mother's nature too.

I sat up as my faery self, felt my ears and checked my fingers to be sure. But I knew: I could see and hear and smell again. I built my own air mirror, and summoned light to see myself, fingered my nose to make sure it felt the same as it looked. Ahhh.

I shifted to my owl-self.

"Wait," said Golden. "Where are you going?"

"The inn."

"Haven't you done enough for one night?"

"No." I flew through the brilliant night to the Feather Inn, taking joy from everything about my owl self. I feasted on the way on mice I tracked by tiny sounds and slaughtered with talons and beak.

I perched in a tree outside the circle of torchlight by the inn.

I feared to make this change. First I let myself be the faery Owl I knew and had been since birth. Remember. I looked at my green clothes. Had I ever seen a human wear such a slashed-sleeve tunic, such an elegant mage-embroidered cloak with warmth spells sewn into it, and such trews and shoes? No. While I still had my own skills and powers, I changed my garments' cloth so it was rough and brown, turned what was river leather about me into something coarser. I climbed from the tree, leaned against its trunk, took a last look and smell around, and sought my other self.

I opened my eyes to a muffled, hidden, freezing world. I shivered. Would the stable be warmer?

"Wait."

I glanced down. Something large, dark, four-legged, and furred stood beside me.

"You'll need money," my teacher said. He was a wolf, and he spoke wolf, but even as this foreign self, I could understand him. A mercy. He dropped a sack that jingled at my feet. "You must be cautious, Owl. Take a few coins out before you go among them. Offer only one at a time in exchange for food or shelter or whatever else you can buy. Never show them you have more; they kill each other for silver, even such false silver as this, which will last only a day. They won't know it is false, but remember, you must not be here when it disappears. Do you have your knife?"

I touched my sheathed dagger, which was made of fire-mountain glass.

"They will have iron," he said.

I shivered. I had seen what iron could do to us. A faery man I knew had a shrivelled hand because he had touched iron. One of my aunts had died of poisoning from the touch of a nail. Stories of other iron-caused unhealing wounds and maimings wandered the usual route of So They Say.

"It may not hurt you. It may be that your father has given you immunity, especially in that shape. If you see iron, test it. Put your hand near it. If you take no hurt of it, that's good to know. That will give you a power underground," he muttered almost to himself. "Tell them as little as possible. Don't trust them. I will wait here."

"Thank you." I took six silvers from the sack of coins, slipped them into my side pocket, and tucked the moneybag into my belt at the back, beneath my cloak. Stumbling a little, I made my way through the thin screen of trees into the muddy, churned, and torchlit inn yard. Most of the mud had frozen into ruts and peaks and hoofprints. It crackled as I crossed it. I went straight to the stable and peered in over the half-door. No cock cried. No mouse squeaked. But a dog tied by the back door of the inn barked at me as I puzzled over the stable doorlatch, a wooden latch threaded through with rope. It didn't rise when I touched it.

Two stableboys came from the tack room, one chewing on something that smelled like bread and hot meat—half of it was still in his hand, wrapped in a dirty cloth. "What is it?" asked the other, who was taller but no less dirty. Both had straw in their hair.

I smiled, pleased that this, too, was a language I could still understand, even though I had changed into this lesser form. I had learned it along the roads. "I'd like to see the horses," I said.

"Why?"

Why? Wouldn't anyone? "Because they're horses."

"Are you daft?"

"No."

The boys looked at each other. "You just want to see them?" said the chewing boy.

"Perhaps touch them?" I said.

The chewing boy swallowed, peered at me. "Dick, you go on back to supper. I'll deal with this," he said.

"All right, Robin," said the taller one, and he went into the tack room.

Robin let me into the stable. "Where're you from, then?"

"The forest."

"And you want to see horses."

"Yes."

"You ever curried one?"

"Never."

"Would you like to?"

"Oh, yes."

He took another bite of his dinner, ducked into the tack room, returned minus what he had been eating, but with two brushes. "Show you on Bess, if you like. Got a stranger's horse here that needs tending after that, and I could use some help." He led me into a stall with a big brown horse in it. She was warm and smelled large and animal, sweaty and a little musty. She looked at us, lowered her nose to smell me. Her breath was hot and hay-sweet, and her whiskers tickled my face.

"Horse," I whispered. I held out my hand and she snuffled it. Her nostrils flared.

"You can touch her. What's your name, then?"

"Owl," I said before I thought. Golden hadn't cautioned me against giving my name this time, but he'd told me about it often enough in other circumstances. Would this boy know the power of names?

"That's a funny name. Here, Owl, stroke her nose like this, but then let's get on with it."

I ran my hand down the bony ridge of the horse's nose. She pressed against my hand.

"Come on." He handed me a brush and we moved farther back. He showed me how to brush Bess, how to look at which way the hair lay and brush with it instead of against it. It whorled some places and switched directions. "Don't be afraid to brush her hard. She likes it."

He left me at it and ran away for a moment, then came back with wide-toothed combs and taught me to comb the horse's mane and tail. "Watch her back hooves. Don't pull too hard or she'll kick you. Okay?"

"Yes. Thank you, Robin."

"Eh. All right. You just keep working on Bess, and I'll finish my supper. When I'm done I'll show you the next job, eh?"

He went away and left me with the horse. I taught myself what she was as I stroked her. She let me touch her everywhere, so long as she knew what I was doing and I didn't startle her. She let me hug her around the neck. She taught me a few words of her language: yes, no, oh, more of that, I like it! Horse. At last. I brushed her until she shone, then leaned against her side, my head to her ribcage, and listened to her heart. Could I be this?

"Here, now," said Robin behind me in a testy voice. "What are you doing?"

I straightened. "Resting." I had found no echoes of horse

inside myself. Maybe that was a problem with this shape: maybe I couldn't sense such things when I was in human form. Or maybe I had no horse in me to awaken.

I looked down at my hands. In one I still held the bristle-and-wood brush, but in the other I held the metal comb. My hand tightened on it. Was it not iron? I let it fall, stared into my palm, which was whole, unmarked. I might have no horse in me, but I had enough human to protect me from the doom of cold iron.

Robin walked around Bess, nodding. "Good. You did good. You sure this is the first time you've touched a horse?"

"Yes."

"No fear in you, is there?"

I looked at him. I had many fears.

"Ah," said Robin. "Well, not scared of horses, anyway, are you?"

"No."

"Good. Let me show you Bruiser."

I followed him to a stall at the end of the stable. We were greeted by a cascade of thunks as the horse inside kicked the walls. "Here's the thing. We've given him food and water," Robin said, "but we haven't brushed him. He doesn't like us. Come up here." He climbed up a ladder to the hayloft. I followed him. "Now take a look." We edged over to look down into Bruiser's stall, and he stared up at us, whites visible in his eyes. He was tall and dark, with a white blaze on his forehead and one white stocking. He screamed and kicked the wall.

"Dick was all for letting you in with him to start," Robin said.

I glanced at him and thought about that. Suppose this was the first horse I had tried to touch? I wouldn't have gone into that stall, though. I'd seen other creatures with bad tempers. I knew enough to stay away. "Something hurts him?"

"Huh. Could be. Just figured he was a bad one, or has a bad master. He's old. Had a hard life. You can see it in his hide." He studied the horse, who stared up at us. "They don't pay us enough to take good care of one like this," Robin said. "It's as much as your life's worth to open that stall. We can leave him. He'll do."

The stable door opened. "Boys!"

Robin and I climbed down the ladder, and Dick came out of the tack room at the far end of the stable. An older man stood at the door, holding two horses by the reins below their chins.

"Well, here," said Robin, "a job to do. Get you some more experience, eh, Owl?"

"Oh, yes."

DICK SNORTED AND TENDED TO ONE HORSE, WHILE ROBIN taught me the intricacies of bridle straps and buckles and saddle girths and blankets, how to rub a sweating horse down with a cloth before brushing it, and how to give only a little water at first to an animal that had been running, and add more later.

Everything we did satisfied something in me that had gone hungry for a long time.

Who was Robin? Why had he decided to be nice to me? With most of the people I knew, I had to claim kinship before they would even speak to me, and then we had to figure out who had more skills and powers so we knew who was above, and who below. Politics were thick in the air at the faery court.

Another reason I liked working with Golden aboveground was that we didn't have to concern ourselves with matters of status except his as teacher and mine as student.

Golden had warned me to be wary of humans. I tried to keep that in mind, but mostly I lost myself in the work, the wonder that I was finally able to touch a horse. Its body heat and hair, coiled power and speed and stamina, lay under my hands and brush.

When we had finished feeding, watering, and brushing the horse, and stored his tack on a numbered stand in the tack room that matched the number of his stall, we went back to the stall with Bruiser in it.

A cat walked along the stall railing. "Who's this, who's this?" she asked, studying me with large yellow eyes. Bruiser kicked the wall below her, and she clung with her claws before she leapt to the straw near me. "What's wrong with you?" she snarled toward the horse, who kicked the wall again.

I knelt and held out a hand to her. She came and sniffed, stared into my eyes, did not recognize me, though I knew her: she was the one who had told me to find a safer scent. "What is wrong with him?" I asked.

The cat blinked. She looked toward the stall.

The horse peered out at us over the top of the stall door.

"He's wrong-eyed," Robin said. "Come on, Owl, there's nothing we can do for him, wild as he is. Let's leave him. Want some tea?"

"You," whispered the horse to me. "You."

I rose.

"Where have you been? The old man took you away from me all those years ago, and you never came back! Where have you been?"

I walked to the stall, one slow step at a time.

"Boy," whispered the horse.

I held out my hand to him.

"Don't! He'll bite it off!" Robin cried, but the horse only smelled me. Then he screamed and whirled away and kicked the wall with both hind feet.

"Not my boy. Not my boy," he muttered, then stood, head hanging, breathing loudly, all his legs stiff.

I leaned on the stall door. "Did you know my father?"

Slowly his head rose. Slowly he stepped to the door, smelled me carefully, nibbled my hair. "Where is he?" he asked.

"No one knows."

"I'll take you, then."

"Will you?" I opened the stall door and slipped in, though Robin cried out to stop me.

The horse trembled as I touched him, but he didn't bite or kick me. His hindquarters were scored with whip marks. I still had a brush in my hand. I showed it to him, and he smelled it, then lipped it, then turned so I could brush him. "Who owns you now?" I asked. He had not been brushed in a long, long time. His hair was matted: layers of sweat, old shed hair, and the start of his winter coat made his hide a nightmare. Cold mud coated his lower legs. Scars old and new marred his hide. The corners of his mouth were thick with callus. Burrs and tangles hung in his mane.

"No one," he said.

Robin brought me a bucket with warm water in it, two rags, a comb, a hoofpick. The horse quieted as I cared for him the way Robin had taught me. Dick came to watch and jeer, but when the horse kicked the wall nearest him, he went away again.

"Who owns him?" I asked Robin.

"Owl, you spoke to him, and he made answers."

"Mm."

"Did you understand him?"

"Ah," I said. I thought: I had started to understand with Bess and the other horse, but everything Bruiser said was as clear to me as though I were talking to Golden or my mother. "Don't you talk to them?" I had watched all matters of the stable from a distance until now, but with the enhanced sight of the owl, the enhanced scent perception of the wolf. I had seen stable boys talking to horses, and men talking to horses as they rode. Had I revealed more about myself than I had planned?

"Course I do," said Robin. "They like the sound of a voice, if it's calm. Soothes them right down sometimes."

"Who owns him?"

"Who did he say when you asked him that?"

"No one."

"Hah!" said Robin. "Caught you."

"What?"

"He does answer, and you do understand. How is that?"

"Who owns him?" I asked for the third time. Underground, anyone who was asked a question three times had to answer with something like truth. There were many ways of turning questions away or changing subjects before the question could be asked a third time. Robin was skilled at this game too, I thought, but still, I had asked. Would he answer?

"A man in the inn brought him, but last I heard, he was offering to sell him for a fraction of his worth, could you but get the horse to cooperate. Now that he's done up so nice, maybe the man will find some buyers."

"I'll buy him."

"Sure! A ragamuffin like you? Didn't you come here looking for work?"

I smiled at him. "I'll be back."

I had never been in a human building other than the stable, but I had seen people go in and out of the inn. Some went in through a door at the back, and some went in through the front. Most travelers, once they had handed their horses over to be taken care of or seen to their horses' stabling themselves, went in through the front door.

I took the brush, bucket, rags, and hoofpick back to the tack room and stowed them where I had seen Robin get them from before. Then I crossed the inn yard and went around the front of the building. My breath made white ghosts as I walked, and my face burned with cold.

The noise of voices, heat, and smoke came out of the door when I opened it, and music: rough song and rougher playing on some instrument with strings, and the yeasty smell of beer, sharp overtones of wine, roasted meat, baked bread, smoke from fire and tobacco. People crowded around tables and the bar in a big, noisy, ill-lit room to the left. It looked more like the sort of party dwarves would throw than any I had seen underground; our gathering rooms were bigger, with taller ceilings, and the people wore better clothes and didn't smell so bad.

The entry hall led past it, with hooks on the wall where people had hung cloaks, now gently steaming in the heat from two separate fireplaces in the common room; a closed door stood to the right, and there was a staircase straight ahead that the hall hooked past.

I had several moments to panic before anyone in the room noticed me. Here I was, inside a human dwelling, near a bunch of humans, most of them bigger than I was, and I had shed my skills and powers. What if they wished me harm?

Mostly they seemed happy with their meat and drink and each other. Laughter boomed. The song the minstrel sang was a funny one, and many joined in the chorus.

A thin man in an apron came to meet me. "Young sir, what's your pleasure?" he asked.

"I heard someone here wants to sell a horse, the big noisy horse in the stable."

"Gallo," he called over his shoulder. A big man in brown fur came away from the bar. "Horse buyer," said the inn keeper before he plunged back into the common room.

"Truly? You're interested in that brute of a — that wonderful creature of mine out back?"

"He looks strong."

"That he is, young sir. He can kick through a stable wall in — he can pull a heavy load. He only wants a bit of handling. Are you good with a whip?"

"How much do you want for him?"

"Thirty silver pieces," he said.

"Oh." I didn't know how many pieces of false silver Golden had given me, and he had told me not to show them in public. How was I supposed to get to them to count them out?

"Don't look so crestfallen, young sir. Tonight could be your lucky night. I've just had a good run of cards, and I'm feeling generous. How about twenty?"

I bit my lip and stared at the floor, wondering if he would

go lower. It didn't matter to me how many he asked for, so long as I had enough. But apparently indecision was part of the game.

"Fifteen, then, but that's final."

"Hey, Gallo! Ten minutes ago you were saying you'd let the monster go for ten!" yelled someone in the room.

Gallo turned and snarled at the other man, then faced me again. "I'll give him to you for ten, though it hurts my heart to let him go so cheap."

"Ten," I said. "Excuse me a moment." I ducked down the hallway until it turned, took out my purse and counted out ten pieces of silver, then returned and handed them to him.

He bit them, studied them, smiled. "Will you want tack, then?" asked Gallo. "I'll throw in his saddle and bridle for another two."

Would the horse want to be saddled and bridled? I wouldn't, if I were a horse. But maybe I should take the tack anyway. I could always throw it away later.

"That tack he's got is only worth half a silver," called the same man in the common room.

I dug one silver out of my pocket and gave it to Gallo. "Will that do?"

"Yes." He tucked the silvers I had given him in his own pocket, then spat in his palm. "Spit to seal our bargain."

I spat in my own palm, and he pressed my hand to his, palm to palm, and squeezed.

"He's all yours, God help you," he said. "All of you are witnesses!"

The nearest people in the common room laughed and nodded and waved mugs of beer at us.

"Thank you." I had a horse. I had a horse. I ran out of the inn to the stables. I had a horse!

Now what?

"You did it?" Robin asked when I entered. "You bought him?"

"Yes. And his tack."

"His tack! Hah! It's worthless. The girth is nearly worn through, the saddle's scuffed to pieces, and the reins are almost past mending."

"Oh, well. I don't imagine I'll be using it much."

"What are you going to do with him?"

"Take him home, if he'll come." Would he come? Down through the gate and into the underground? What would my mother say if I brought a horse home? We had room in our house for a horse, but if my mother didn't like him, perhaps it was time for me to carve out my own living space.

If the horse wouldn't come through the gate, what was I going to do with him?

Dick brought me a very sorry saddle, a thin saddle pad, and sad reins with tarnished buckles and a heavy, sharp bit. If I were a horse, I wouldn't want to wear any of this, especially that bit. It would cut the tongue.

Once I was myself again, I could fix these things if I wanted to, make them remember what they had been like when they were new and fine, if they ever had been. I went to Bruiser's stall and opened the door. He glanced at me. "Did you eat enough?"

He went back to the food bin and ate the grain I had put there, drank deep from the bucket. How was I going to feed him?

"You want me to help you put the tack on him?" Robin asked.

I looked at the degenerate bits of things in my hands. "I don't think he'd like it."

"How are you going to ride him, then?"

"Ride him?" I hadn't thought this through. "But I don't know how to ride."

"I suppose it's just as well, that brute. Probably wouldn't let you stay on him anyway. What do you want him for, then?"

"I don't know." I walked toward the stable door, and Bruiser followed me. "Robin, thanks for everything."

"Hey. Come back if you want work, Owl. I'm sure they'd hire you. You learn fast, and you're good with the animals."

"Thanks." We passed Dick, who leaned, arms crossed, against Bess's stall door. Then we were outside in the flicker-torch dark and cold. I led my horse out of the yard into the forest.

He snorted and reared when we came to where Golden waited.

"It's all right, horse. This is my teacher. He won't hurt you."

"Won't I?" asked Golden, who was still a wolf. "Why have you gotten this animal, Owl?"

"It's what I've always wanted, Teacher. You know that. This is my horse."

"This is my boy," said the horse.

"Oh ho," said Golden.

"Horse," I said, "I'm going to change now so we can get home before daybreak. Only — "

"What'll you do, Owl? Fly off and leave the creature behind?" Golden asked.

"How far do you have to go?" asked the horse.

"A league and a half."

"Climb on my back," said the horse.

I studied the saddle, saddle pad, and bridle I held, wondered if they would help me. I climbed up into a tree and left them on a branch, then lowered myself onto the horse's back. He stayed steady. His back was broad.

It was strange to be shaped like I was and this high off the ground on top of something that moved.

"Boy, hug my neck," the horse said. "Wolf, lead the way."

The horse carried me through the night all the way to the gate. I clung to his huge hard warmth, my cheek pressed to his neck, his coarse mane whipping against my face and shoulders as he ran, my legs splayed wider apart than was comfortable. I was shaky and rattled by the time we reached our destination, but elated, too: the horse had let me ride him, given me a way into one of his mysteries.

"Thank you," I said. I let myself down off his back and collapsed, my legs too wobbly to hold me.

The horse nibbled my hair. "You'll have to learn better than that," he said.

"You mean we can do it again?"

"Yes."

"Oh, thank you." I stretched out on my back and reached for my other self. It didn't take me so long to find it this second time. I wrapped myself in change, felt the arcane strengths and skills come back to me. The world of scents came alive to me, and my hearing sharpened. I felt the breeze stroke my face and hands. Better. Much better. I ran my hand through my hair and sat up.

"Who are you?" cried the horse.

"I'm Owl," I said.

"You're not! You're not my boy's son anymore!" He reared, pawed the air, backed away from me.

"I am," I said.

"No! Nothing about you tastes or smells like him! Imposter. You tricked me!"

"Horse," I cried. I held out my hand. He danced away, plunged, kicked out. Golden dove, knocked me over before the horse could fell me.

The horse ran away into the frozen forest.

Light washed the edge of the sky. Winter's edge chilled the tears on my face. Golden shifted away from wolf, rose as his faery self, picked me up, carried me through the gate and home.

After I had slept, my mother made me dress in my best clothes and took me to a celebration in the queen's court. The warmth was just right in the spacious room, and all the colors bright and clean and pleasing to the eye. The smells were light and delicious, some of them flowers, some of them food; ripe fruit, light cakes. Minstrels played, and many danced; those of us who didn't dance, sat by rank at tables, and ate and drank and talked.

All the children of my generation were there, seated beside their mothers, dressed well and looking like younger, less troubled versions of the elders.

Golden was not there. He hated affairs such as this.

I sat beside my sister-friend, Henna. The halfbloods, those

who were not my siblings and wore their humanity openly instead of hidden against their spines, moved among us, offering fruit and sweets on green glass trays. Everyone ate. Everyone acted as though the trays floated past them unsupported by visible beings.

I touched one serving girl's wrist, and she paused, her yellow eyes wide, and looked down at me. Her ears were as pointed as any of ours, her eyes as slanted, her chin as sharp; but she smelled human. She bowed so low her wrist slipped out of my grasp, and then she hurried away.

Henna stared at me.

We were not supposed to notice them. We were not supposed to touch them. They were only allowed among us by grace. They should be thankful they were here in faery halls, instead of grubbing in the dirt above. These half-human lesser beings —

Half human. Who was I to condemn them?

I blinked, gazed around the great hall, saw suddenly half again as many people present. Those of us who stood, carried trays, walked among the seated, slipped past the dancing ones—

More faery than I had looked when I saw my father's face in Golden's mirror.

I did not know the names of any of them. I saw the girl I had touched, standing against the wall, whispering to an older boy with round ears. She glanced toward me, dropped her gaze.

Where did they go when they were not serving us? What did they do? Were they kind to strangers, as Robin had been kind?

If I wanted to talk to one of them, I would have to find her sometime when no one else was around. I didn't know if that was even possible, but it might be a thing worth trying.

It might be easier if I looked like my father.

I turned back to my sister-friend. The skills Henna studied involved weaving: she wove light, water, air, and fire, and sometimes words and music into cloth, spells, food. Had she ever thought about our father? Had it ever occurred to her that he, too, had been a weaver, as he, too, had been a shapeshifter? Did she ever realize he had been human under everything our dead king had done to give him the power to sire us? Had she ever asked her mother or her teacher what he looked like?

"Come aboveground with me tonight," I whispered to her during a burst of laughter. Henna was the best of my friends, my favorite sister. I wanted to talk to her about what it meant to be children of our father.

She did not answer me until some time had passed.

But at last she said, "All right."

Perhaps the horse would come back, and I could introduce him to another of my father's children. Perhaps she would smell right; I knew I could smell right again.

I did not know what to hope for, but I hoped.

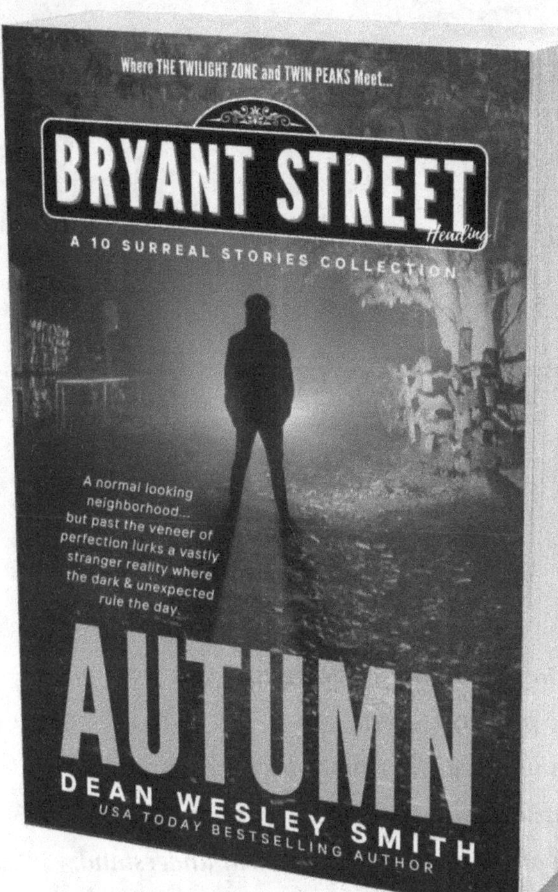

Where THE TWILIGHT ZONE and TWIN PEAKS Meet...
BRYANT STREET
Hendling
A 10 SURREAL STORIES COLLECTION
A normal looking neighborhood... but past the veneer of perfection lurks a vastly stranger reality where the dark & unexpected rule the day.
AUTUMN
DEAN WESLEY SMITH
USA TODAY BESTSELLING AUTHOR

Where
THE TWILIGHT ZONE
Lives...
wmgbooks.com

Where THE TWILIGHT ZONE and TWIN PEAKS Meet...
BRYANT STREET
A 10 SURREAL STORIES COLLECTION
A normal looking neighborhood... but past the veneer of perfection lurks a vastly stranger reality where the dark & unexpected rule the day.
SUMMER
DEAN WESLEY SMITH
USA TODAY BESTSELLING AUTHOR

Where THE TWILIGHT ZONE and TWIN PEAKS Meet...
BRYANT STREET
A 10 SURREAL STORIES COLLECTION
WINTER
DEAN WESLEY SMITH
USA TODAY BESTSELLING AUTHOR

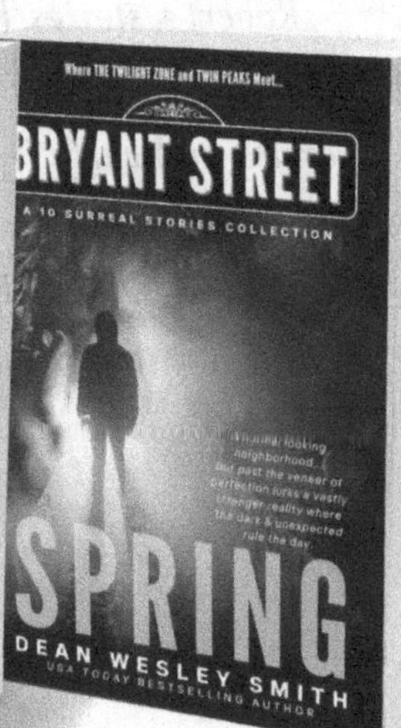

Where THE TWILIGHT ZONE and TWIN PEAKS Meet...
BRYANT STREET
A 10 SURREAL STORIES COLLECTION
A normal looking neighborhood... but past the veneer of perfection lurks a vastly stranger reality where the dark & unexpected rule the day.
SPRING
DEAN WESLEY SMITH
USA TODAY BESTSELLING AUTHOR

ROBERT JESCHONEK

Robert Jeschonek continues his streak of being in every issue of this magazine. All thirty-two plus Issue Zero.

The reason Robert has this streak is simply because his stories are often just perfect Pulphouse stories. Take this story, for example. Just read the first paragraph about the dog and you will understand. Have fun!

Robert's stories have appeared in dozens of magazines and he has published dozens of novels as well. He has even worked for DC Comics and early in his career sold me a couple stories when I was editing for Star Trek at Pocket Books. He seems to be able to do it all. And to see all the amazing projects he has done, check out his website at https://www.robertjeschonek.com/

DOG AND PONY SHOW

ROBERT JESCHONEK

People say the needles of a dog are a boy's best friend, and I believe them.

I mean, the nozzles are okay, too, and I shiver with delight when they unfold from my dog Wazoo's gleaming carapace. I love when they spray the green gas that makes me work harder, or the purple gas that makes the daydreams come.

But the *needles* are the *most* magic part of the dog. Just ask anyone.

One minute, I'm collapsed on the concrete floor of my bin, exhausted from another triple shift of Playtime. The next minute, ol' Wazoo is scuttling over to me on his six spiny black legs, barking sweetly.

K-klak klik buzzzz klak klik.

Right away, as tired as I am, I'm smiling again. I can't help it. My pup always takes good care of me.

As his glossy black face gazes down at me, shiny silver

needles poke out from the hundreds of facets in his big, bulbous eyes. When he leans closer, they jab into my nose, and I smell his voice in my mind, singing a story of very strong perfume like the scent given off by rotting flesh. Can there be anything more soothing to a ten-year-old boy like me, living with the perfect dog in the paradise of Beastbless, in the parish of Menagerie?

Among dog lovers, this is what we call a good nose-lick. And it is enough, all alone, to make life worth living.

———

DO YOU KNOW HOW LUCKY I AM TO HAVE A DOG AT ALL? OR A dog as great as Wazoo? My same-aged friend, Incompleta, would do *anything* to have Wazoo or any dog like him.

This morning, she reminds me again. "Are you sure you don't want to trade your dog for my breakfast, Beneathy?"

"Thanks, but I already have breakfast." From across the gray table where we eat alongside dozens of fellow Play-timers, I hold up my bowl of delicious red morning clay, sweetened with a garnish of baby chicks. As adorable as they are delicious, the chicks' tiny black bodies scurry around on eight spindly legs, trying to avoid my white plastic spoon.

"I have another idea." She reaches back over her right shoulder, and two long, rust-colored antennae brush her hand. "We could trade *my* pet for *your* pet." The body of a young kitten flows over her shoulder, hundreds of tiny legs flickering under its segmented scarlet shell. The body just keeps coming, wrapping around her three times like a gleaming stole.

"Lovebite *is* adorable." I reach over to pet the kitten's smooth head, laughing as it snaps at me with its jagged pincers.

Incompleta puts her hand under the kitten's mouth, which disgorges a glob of lumpy green ooze. "Just listen to her purr."

"I hear it," I tell her, and I do. *Screee snap shrreee snap screeee.* "What a beautiful sound," I say, though I still believe there's nothing as sweet as the bark of a dog. "Are you serious about trading her? Why would you ever give her up?"

"Because dogs are just the best." Her freckled face reddens as she stares at Wazoo, who then scuttles down off my back and under the table. Lovebite's tail scrolls around Incompleta's head, little legs fluttering through her short red hair. "And *yours* is the best *ever.*"

She's right about that. Smiling, I reach under the table to feel Wazoo's bristly proboscis quivering, making my fingertips sticky. I wouldn't know what to do if I ever lost him; I can hardly remember what life was like before I got him.

"So will you trade him for my kitty?" asks Incompleta.

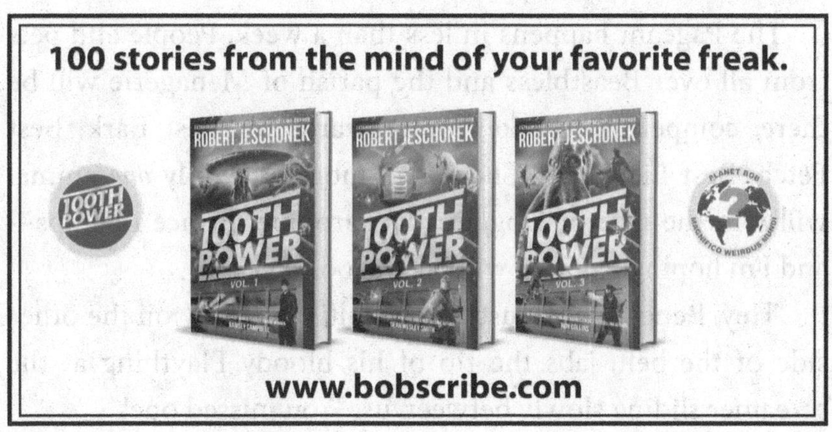

"No way." I smile as Wazoo hops and barks, bumping the underside of the table. *K-klak klik buzzzz klak klik.*

Incompleta sighs. "I wouldn't, either. Especially with the dog shortage going on."

"There's a shortage?" I spoon scuttling baby chicks and red clay into my mouth and chew.

"That's right." As Incompleta eats the lumpy green ooze, her darling Lovebite rears its head up and jabs a clear spike into the soft spot on top of her skull, sipping pink fluid from her head. I'm a little jealous; as great as dogs are, a cat can still be pretty cute when it's bonding with its owner. "And you better keep a close eye on *your* dog if you don't want to end up at the Pet Pageant empty-handed."

I think about the Pet Pageant a lot during Playtime. It helps take my mind off the screaming things on the Funsembly Line as my fellow Playtimers and I make them extra Beautiful and Happy.

The Pageant happens in less than a week. People and pets from all over Beastbless and the parish of Menagerie will be there, competing to take home awards for Best Bark, Best Fetch, Best Lick, Best Chew, and more. But only *one* animal will win the title of Doggiest Dogaroonie, Prince of Pups— and I'm hoping *that* dog will be Wazoo.

"Hey, Beneathy!" Caustico, the tall, blond boy on the other side of the belt, jabs the tip of his bloody Plaything at the screamer sliding slowly between us. "You missed one!"

Snapping out of my reverie, I instantly spot what he's

talking about and jump to fix it. The screamer shrieks at the top of his lungs as I leave my playful mark on his belly, getting him ready for the next level of the Playtime game.

"You wanna *win* this time, or not?" snaps Caustico.

"Sure I do."

"Then pay attention." Caustico flicks blood at me from his Plaything. It will blend right in with my red coveralls and the other blood already soaked into them. "We're supposed to be on the same team, remember?" He puts down the Plaything and reaches for a Joy Stick, its barbed tip cherry-red and smoking.

"I will, I will." Even as I say it, my mind drifts back to the only thing I really want to win. I imagine my wonderful dog atop the Hill of Buddies, barking and flashing his glossy black wings as the top judge drapes a gold medal around his proboscis. I can just see Wazoo flapping up into the air and flying victory laps above the crowd, that beautiful medal swinging and glinting in the sunlight.

K-klak klik buzzzz klak klik.

On the front of the gleaming gold medal is the image of a dog's face, complete with multifaceted eyes with needles jutting out of each facet. Two words are emblazoned around the edge of the medal, following the curved edge:

Doggiest Dogaroonie.

I see a date, too, and the name of the winner, and I feel a rush of joyful warmth from head to toe. As wonderful as every day of my life is, as lucky as I have always been to be alive and here, this one thing is what I most long to see.

According to the medal in my daydream, the name of the winning dog is Wazoo, and this year is when he will win the title of Doggiest Dogaroonie.

THE BUNNIES ARE BITING OUTSIDE WHEN I TAKE WAZOO FOR A walk after Playtime. Clouds of them swirl around us, tiny dark flecks getting in my eyes and nipping at my skin—making me smile with each tiny bite, because who doesn't love bunnies and their tender little kisses?

Wazoo, as usual, scuttles back and forth before me, probing black masses and smears left behind by other pets on the sidewalk. Once in a while, he gets excited and pops out his wings, shooting pink mist from the special white nozzles exposed along his back. The mist, which smells sweet like burning plastic and drying paint, always makes me feel a little tipsy when I get a whiff of it.

Suddenly, Wazoo stops zigzagging and bolts off the sidewalk on a beeline. He drags me along behind him through the brush, holding on to his prickly leash for dear life.

"What are you doing, boy?" I duck out of the way of a low-hanging branch that narrowly misses my head. "Where are you going?'"

Wazoo, who has never done anything like this before, answers by buzz-snorting and picking up speed, rushing even more recklessly onward. I stumble on a rock, then trip on a root, nearly going down both times—but miraculously stay on my feet.

K-klak klik buzzzz klak klik.

Wazoo's barks get louder the further off-trail we go. The loudest comes when he hurtles into a clearing and stops. When I stumble in behind him, I see why.

Wazoo isn't a big fan of complete strangers, and the clearing is full of them. Three cops in standard gray uniforms encircle a crouching man and a little boy, younger than me, on his knees.

When the cops hear us, they move apart enough for me to see that the boy is crying and cradling something in his arms… something so misshapen, I can't figure out what it is.

K-klak klik buzzzz klak klik.

Bzzzzeeeeeekkk.

I've never heard Wazoo bark like that before, like some kind of broken machine. His wings unfold, and he takes to the air; I have to let go of the leash as he flies circles around the strangers in the clearing.

"What's going on here?" The words rush out of me, though I feel like I'm intruding.

The boy's face is wet with tears and smudged with black as he looks up at me. Moving closer, I see by the fading light that his arms are full of broken pieces of something black and shiny. Multicolored fluids drip from his elbows and run down his knees, pooling in the dirt.

His father drops a hand on his shoulder, but the boy only sobs harder. "W-who would *do* something like this?" The boy asks the question as if I know the answer. "Who would k-kill my sweet Gilgamog?"

Only when he says it and holds out the broken pieces do I realize what has happened here. Only then do I understand what has been in his arms since before I arrived.

And my heart sinks. My belly twists, and I want to run away that very second. "Your poor dog…"

"I loved her with all my *h-heart*," says the boy. "And now somebody *k-killed* her!"

"Somebody or some*thing*," corrects one of the cops, a male.

"We don't know which one yet," says a female cop.

"It doesn't matter." The boy slumps to the ground on his side, still clutching the broken pieces of his beloved dog. His voice grows soft as he shivers with sobs. "She's d-dead. My dog is *d-dead*."

Meanwhile, Wazoo keeps circling overhead, making that new sound as he passes.

Bzzzzeeeeeekkk.

Bzzzzeeeeeekkk.

Bzzzzeeeeeekkk.

PEOPLE SAY THE WORLD WOULD BE A DARK AND AWFUL PLACE without the Nylon Knights around to keep it bright. Seeing them ride into town the next morning atop their handsome steeds, I believe it.

The seven men and women ride tall in the saddle, clad in gleaming white plastic armor from head to toe. The long lances they carry are just as perfectly white, and so are the saddles they sit on. Proud and strong, the Knights stare straight ahead, fixed on their mission with unwavering focus.

Their legendary horses are just as impressive. Their long green bodies clamber down the street, perfectly balanced and nimble on slender legs though they hardly look sturdy enough to carry the weight of armored riders. With spiny forelegs always folded, they look like they're constantly begging or praying—though the truth is, those legs can swing and clamp suddenly in time of battle.

Who could resist running over to touch such beautiful animals? Not me. Along with a dozen other young Playtimers, I hurry over on the way to the Funsembly Line and pet the bright green hide of the closest horse. The hide is one of the nicest things I've ever touched, studded with points and bumps and jagged burs that prick my skin and draw blood. It feels so good, I could gladly pet it for the rest of the day, if I had time.

HSSSSS. As the horse whinnies, its triangular head spins around, and its big green eyes look my way. *HSSSKLAK.*

"They're so pretty!" Incompleta is beside me, stroking the leafy green folds of the horse's wing. "I wish *I* had a pony like this!"

"Is there any animal you *don't* want?" I ask her.

"A giraffe, maybe," she tells me. "Too many *fangs* and too much *venom*, you know?"

Just then, the Knight spurs the horse, and it trots out of reach. We move on to the next in line, which turns out to have an even nicer hide. Two strokes along its leg, and my hand is speckled with blood.

Impetuous as ever, Incompleta shouts up at the Nylon Knight. "Why are you here? Is it because of the dog killer?"

The Knight, a woman, judging from the cut of its armor, glances down at us. Two eyes glow bright red from the dark-ness under her visor—and then a third glows bright yellow between them. "Curfew begins now." Her voice is a droning monotone. "Proceed to your Playhouse and lock yourselves inside until further notice."

"Do you know who's taking and killing the pets?" asks Incompleta. "Do you know where to find him?"

"Information later," says the Knight. "Curfew begins now." With that, she spurs her horse, which rears up and whinnies before galloping off with the rest of the team.

HSSSSS. HSSSKLAK.

Incompleta sighs. "I want a pony more than *ever* now."

"Have you ever thought of becoming a Nylon Knight?" I

ask as Wazoo scuttles up between us. "Then you'd get a pony for sure."

"Only if I get to keep Lovebite." She pats her shoulder, and the long red kitten crawls up her back from under her shirt and wraps itself around her head like a multi-legged, segmented turban. "And a dog like Wazoo, of course. And maybe a giraffe, after all. Wearing a Knight's super-hard plastic armor would make its poisonous fangs easier to deal with, wouldn't it?"

THERE'S NO LAW AGAINST LEAVING PLAYTIME EARLY BECAUSE who would want to? The Funsembly Line is just what the name says—fun to the *max*.

But today, for the first time in my life, leaving early is exactly what I do. I leave *three hours* early, believe it or not.

And it's all because of Incompleta and her cat.

"Beneathy! You've got to help me!" She dashes into the room in a frantic state, eyes wide and hair wild. "Lovebite is gone!"

I admit, I'm annoyed at the interruption. The screamer on the belt is in peak shriek, and I've got a fired-up Joy Stick with his name on it. "Gone?"

"She slipped away somehow!" Incompleta grabs my sleeve. "I was busy playing and only just noticed."

"Where could she have gone?"

"Anywhere! You know how cats are!" She shakes my arm roughly, oblivious to all the Playtimers who are staring our way. "Please, Beneathy! Help me find her!"

The screamer's going berserk. I have to finish him ASAP or someone else will get to have all the fun. "She's probably just somewhere in the Playhouse."

"She's *not*," snaps Incompleta. "I've looked *everywhere*. She has to be outside. Maybe she sneaked out through a vent or a crack or something."

"I'm sure she's fine." I shrug off her hand and turn back to the screamer, raising the Joy Stick over his already-flaming navel. "Cats can take care of themselves pretty well."

That's the last straw for Incompleta. With a loud grunt, she knocks the stick from my hand, seizes my arm, and drags me away from the Funsembly Line.

I try to pull away, but she's got a firm grip. Other Play-timers look like they think about helping me, but none of them do.

When we get to the doorway, I grab hold of the jamb and fight, determined to stay put. She responds by swinging me around against the wall and getting up in my face.

"What if it was *your* pet who was missing?" Even as she hisses out the words, Wazoo scurries around us, bumping our legs and barking. "Would you do nothing and just hope he came back?"

K-klak klik buzzzz klak klik.

Wazoo's barks change my mind. So does the memory of the kid from the clearing the night before, the one crying over the broken corpse of the dog called Gilgamog.

Incompleta is right.

I shake my head and stop fighting. "Can somebody cover for me? I need to go look for a cat."

"Sure!" Caustico's only too happy to take my place. "But I

don't think the Nylon Knights make exceptions to the curfew for *cat-finders.*"

"Here, Kitty Kitty!" calls Incompleta as we wander the forest of Beastbless. "Come to Mama, little Lovebite!"

The noise makes me nervous. I keep looking around, worried that the Nylon Knights might hear and punish us for breaking curfew...or worse, that the pet killer might decide to kill something other than pets. Sneaking out of the Playhouse might not have been the smartest move we've ever made.

Though of course I want to find Lovebite, too. I can't stand the thought of any pet owner, especially a fellow Playtimer, going without the sweet companion that makes life worth living.

"Lovebite!" My calls aren't as loud, but at least I bring another helper to the search. Antennae wiggling, Wazoo crashes through the brush by my side, snuffling at the vegetation with his bristly proboscis. If there's one thing a dog's good at, it's hunting down a cat.

"Where *is* she?" Incompleta stomps her foot in frustration. "We keep getting farther from the Playhouse, and there's still no sign of her!"

"Chasing a mouse, probably. Cats can't resist the *claws* and *stingers* on those things." I push through a patch of waist-high weeds, but nothing jumps out at me. Nothing much interests Wazoo, either.

"What if the killer got her?" Incompleta sounds panicky,

and her eyes well up with tears. "What if the reason she's not coming to me is that she's dead?"

"I'll bet she's fine. Cats have nine lives, don't they?" I smile her way with a confidence I don't really feel.

But it's hard to keep up a good front as we search further without success. Either Lovebite's a great hider, a fast traveler, or something's happened to her—an accident or attack by another animal if not the pet killer.

Suddenly, though, Incompleta gets excited. She ducks down at the base of a big tree and picks up a bloody mass of fluff and feathers.

"Look, Beneathy! I'd recognize this dead goldfish anywhere! It's the work of my sweet little Lovebite!"

Just then, we hear a loud animal cry from nearby, followed by the sound of thrashing through the brush, moving rapidly away.

Without a word or hesitation, Incompleta leaps up and bolts away in the direction of the thrashing. I'm about to race off after her when I have a sudden change of plan.

K-klak klik buzzzz klak klik.

Barking his head off, Wazoo charges in the opposite direction, running so hard that he snaps his leash. Whatever he's after, I can't see or even hear it.

But what if he's heading into danger?

I hesitate for an instant, looking one way and then the other. Wazoo and Incompleta might both need my help. Which one do I go after?

Bzzzzeeeeeekkk.

As soon as I hear that sound, the one Wazoo made at the scene of the other dog's murder, my mind is made up. I run after him as fast as I can, leaving Incompleta to her own devices.

Bzzzzeeeeeekkk.

But as I run, and Wazoo keeps making those sounds, I wish I'd brought a Joy Stick from the Playhouse or something else I could use as a weapon. I'm just so used to a world where pets aren't killed, and the only Playtime happens on the Funsembly Line, I didn't even think about it.

Bzzzzeeeeeekkk.

Bzzzzeeeeeekkk.

Bzzzzeeeeeekkk.

But I'm thinking about it now. As I burst into a thicket of trees and see Wazoo face to face with some kind of monster, I'm thinking about it *hard*.

Because the monster, with its four legs, long tail, and mottled brown and black fur, is crouching, baring its gleaming white fangs, and making a noise deep in its throat that can mean only one thing.

Grrrrrrrrrrrrr.

And that one thing is Playtime, monster style.

EARS FLATTENED BACK AGAINST ITS HEAD, THE MONSTER SNAPS its jaws and lets loose an unholy howl.

Raarrrrhh.

My heart's pounding, my hands are shaking—but Wazoo is unfazed. Fanning out his black wings, he roars at the monster with more menace than I've ever seen him muster.

SCREEE KLAK EEEE AAARRKK.

The monster lunges, snapping and howling with wild ferocity.

RAARRRR RARRRR RARRRRR.

Instead of backing down, Wazoo lunges at the monster, spraying green gas from one nozzle and black from another. The monster lurches back, coughing and shaking its head hard.

Wazoo presses the attack, unleashing more plumes of gas. His opponent coughs harder than ever and stumbles back on shaky legs, his savagery flagging.

Just as I cheer in my heart, however, things suddenly change. Loud, heavy footfalls pound toward us, accompanied by violent thrashing. Another monster explodes into the thicket, much bigger than the first—a four-legged beast taller than I am, with glossy black hair and a long face with a bone-white stripe down the middle. Before Wazoo can direct any sprays in its direction, this monster whips around and lashes out with its two hind legs, blasting a brutal kick in his direction.

The new monster's feet land with such force that they propel Wazoo across the thicket into a tree trunk. He slams into the wood and bounces off, dropping into a patch of weeds where he lies motionless on his back, leaking multicolored gases from his nozzles.

"Wazoo!" I start to run to him, but I don't get far. The bigger, black-haired monster lumbers between us, blocking the way.

And then it gets worse. *More* monsters straggle in from all sides of the thicket, closer in size to the first—each covered in fur of a different color yet essentially the same type of creature as the first monster to attack. They all have similar shapes, with stubby snouts, black noses, and tails...and they all make the same noise in their throats as they converge around me.

Grrrrrrrrrrr.

I look around frantically for a way out or a weapon but find neither. I'm trapped and helpless in the midst of monsters who might have just killed my faithful companion.

Grrrrrrrrrr.

The biggest monster with the bone-white face backs out of the way as the other monsters come closer. They let him through, concerned only with me.

"Go away!" I try to sound tough. "Get out of here! Leave me alone!"

It doesn't work. The ring of monsters tightens.

"I said go!" I start to realize this might be it, the end, and I wonder: Is this what happened to the missing and murdered pets?

Suddenly, then, I hear an unexpected sound—a *whistle.* The kind of whistle only a human being can make.

And then a voice. The voice of a boy my age or not much older.

"So tell me." When the boy steps into the thicket, I see he has long blond hair and bright blue eyes. His clothes are very brown, very dirty, or both, and his face and hands are caked with grime. "Should I call off the dogs, or let 'em have you?"

I stare at the growling monsters arrayed around me. "Those aren't dogs," I tell him, though I know I shouldn't talk back, given the circumstances. "I *have* a dog."

The new boy chuckles. "No offense, kid, but you're barking up the wrong damn tree."

The boy, who says his name is Joe, leads me off through the forest with the monsters in tow. If I try to get away, he warns me, the monsters—which he insists on calling "dogs" and a "horse"—will run me down, and I might get hurt.

But otherwise, he promises, hurting me is the last thing he wants to do.

"Then what *do* you want to do to me?" I ask him.

"I want to tell you the truth," says Joe. "Though, to be honest, *that* might hurt a little bit, too."

We walk for what seems like a very long time, weaving between trees and through brush. I keep looking around, hoping I'll see Wazoo zooming to the rescue with nozzles fuming…but all I see are sharks flitting around, chirping, and flapping their colorful, feathered wings. The sight of them with their pointy little beaks makes me shiver, the way sharks always do.

When we come to a little stream, the "dogs" and "horse" stop to drink, their pink tongues lapping up the trickling water amid sunbeams cast down through the treetops. It's sickening; everyone *knows* dogs only get their moisture by sipping it from the bodies of *dead* things.

"You've never spent time with real animals, have you?" Joe runs his hand along the side of the "horse," stroking its glossy black hair. "I'll bet you've never even touched one, have you?"

"You don't know what you're talking about." I know I'm scowling, but I can't help it. I hate him and all his monsters.

"Or maybe *you're* the one who doesn't truly understand." Joe reaches down, and a big "dog" with shaggy golden fur trots over and licks his fingers.

Watching that happen makes my stomach churn. I think I might throw up—but not yet.

Smiling, Joe pats the beast's head, and the "dog's" tail flicks quickly from side to side. "It's not your fault," he tells me. "All you know is what you were taught."

"*You* don't know *anything*."

"But that's all right." Joe whistles, and the "dogs" and

"horse" stop drinking and start across the stream. "You really *can* teach an old dog new tricks, my friend."

———

AFTER A WHILE, WE COME TO AN ANCIENT CABIN AT THE BASE of a tree-lined hillside, which seems to be our destination. The "dogs" run barking to the decrepit front door, and the "horse" ambles over to a rickety water trough for a drink.

"Welcome to camp." Joe claps a hand on my shoulder and leads me toward the ramshackle little building. "Or as I like to call it, Home-for-Now."

The front door opens, and a tall old man looks out from a cloud of wispy white hair. The "dogs" go crazy, jumping on their hind legs and pawing at his torso and chest. "Good boys," he tells them. "Good dogs."

"Hey Grampa!" shouts Joe. "Look what I found!"

"Oh, Joe." Grampa wags his head. "What have I told you about bringing home strays?"

"But he doesn't know what a real *dog* is," says Joe. "He doesn't know about the *old days*."

Grampa eases his way out the door, feeding the jumping "dogs" with chips of black jerky from the pockets of his tattered denim overalls. "He's probably better off that way. The truth *hurts*."

"I already told him about that." Joe guides me forward. "Maybe he can take it."

Eyes narrowed, Grampa stoops and meets my gaze. "The others won't like it when they get back from the hunt. They'll say you shouldn't have brought him here."

"But isn't this why we're doing it?" asks Joe. "For people like him?"

"Doing what?" I frown. "Who are the others, and what are they hunting?"

Grampa shakes his head. "You remember what happened to the last one you brought in?" He isn't speaking to me.

Joe sighs in frustration. "Just *tell* him. Please?"

I've never had anyone stare at me as hard as Grampa does then. He makes me so uncomfortable, I squirm and want to run away.

Reaching into his pocket, he pulls out a two-inch-long strip of jerky. "Take it." When I don't reach for it, he grabs my hand and presses the jerky into my palm. "Now give it to him." He gestures at one of the "dogs"—a little white-and-tan furred one with pointy ears, short legs, and big green eyes. "His name is Stubby."

Stubby scampers toward me, licking his lips. Heart pounding, I jump back and drop the jerky. Stubby gobbles it up and gazes at me, clearly hoping for more.

"Congratulations," says Grampa. "You just fed an actual dog."

Stubby hops up and sniffs my fingers. I wipe them on my pants to try to shed the smell of the jerky, but then he just sniffs and licks my pants.

"Those *other* things," says Grampa. "The ones you and everyone else think of as dogs—they *aren't*." He walks back to the cabin and returns a moment later with a white plastic bag. It crinkles as he opens it and reaches inside. "*This* isn't a *dog.*"

He pulls something out of the bag, and my blood turns icy

cold. I back away when he holds it up to me, stopped only by Joe when he clamps a hand on my shoulder.

"*This* is a *bug*."

Grampa is wrong. I don't care *what* he says. The thing in his hand is *nothing* like a *bug*.

It's a *dog*, a true *dog*, just like Wazoo, complete with a black proboscis, a shiny black shell that opens up into wings, and bulbous eyes with hundreds of facets for popping out the silver needles that are a boy's best friend.

But for once, a dog like this isn't a welcome sight. This one isn't moving. It doesn't make even the slightest twitch, and the reason is clear.

Its body has a gaping hole in it.

"It's dead." A thought occurs to me, and I feel sicker than ever. "You *killed* it, didn't you?"

Grampa doesn't answer my question. "If you tell enough people this is a *dog*, they *accept* that it's a dog." Black bits of the dead dog trickle out as he shakes it emphatically. "They forget what a *real* dog is like. Or a *cat*, or a *horse*. Or a *life*. They forget that things could be different. *Better*."

Grampa tosses the dead dog aside and marches over to grab my arm. He grips it so hard that it hurts.

"But *some* of us remember. And we tend the *packs* and tell the *stories* and wait for the day when the *better* things replace the *ugly* ones."

"Because you kill them!" I twist free of Grampa's grip. Joe makes a grab for me, and I push him away. "That's what you *do*, isn't it? You're the ones who've been killing the pets!"

"They aren't pets," says Grampa. "They're monsters. They're *controlling* you, and you don't even know it."

"Did you kill *my* dog, too? Did you kill Wazoo?"

Grampa stands there, glaring, and shakes his head. "His indoctrination is *deep*, isn't it?" Again, he's talking to Joe, not me. "I don't know if we can ever get through to him."

"That's what you used to say about me, too," says Joe.

"That's true." Grampa's features soften. "Maybe you're right."

"We should take a break, don't you think?" says Joe.

"Sure." Grampa turns and heads for the cabin. He pulls jerky out of his pocket, and the "dogs" come running. "We'll pick it up later."

But as I watch him go, taking a break is the last thing on my mind. If these people killed Wazoo, or even Lovebite, I will *never* see things their way. I will *never* forgive them.

And I will *never* let go of the life and world I know.

"Come on," says Joe. "Let's go play with the puppies."

"Play? Like on the Funsembly Line?" It doesn't make sense. "But I don't have a Joy Stick or Plaything. I don't even have a *man opener*."

"Don't worry." Joe walks off, gesturing for me to come with him. "Different kind of play."

Joe and I hike to a nearby field, followed by a dozen "dogs." The afternoon sun shines bright on the tall grass waving in the warm breeze.

None of which improves my mood a bit. I don't see how anything could, as long as I'm with one of the people who for all I know might have done something terrible to Wazoo.

Seemingly oblivious to how I'm feeling, Joe scouts through the grass, looking for something. "Have you ever played fetch?" he asks.

"With my dog, a *real* dog, yes." I stay close to the treeline, hoping for a chance to slip away.

Joe sees something and ducks down to retrieve it. "Well, that's what we're going to play." He resurfaces with a stick in his hand, fairly straight and about two feet long. "I'll make the first throw, and you can take the one after that."

When he whistles, the "dogs" fling themselves in front of him, jumping around and making noise.

Rarrrr Rarrr Rarrr Rarrrr Rarrrr.

"Fetch!" When he gives the stick a throw, the "dogs" scramble after it, churning pell-mell across the field. One of them, a big white "dog" with black spots and floppy black ears, scoops it away from another "dog" (a little one with gray fur and a pushed-in face) and runs it back to Joe with a spring in his step.

"Good boy! Good boy!" Joe scratches behind the "dog's"

ears and takes the stick. As he reels it up and back for another throw, the spotted "dog" jumps around crazily, never taking his eyes off the thing. As soon as Joe heaves it, the "dog" bolts off after it, joined by several others.

"You ready?" Joe shouts in my direction. "Want to give it a shot?

"That isn't *fetch*," I tell him. "Not enough *fire*."

"There's no fire in *real* fetch." When Joe gets the stick back, he throws it my way. "Now you try."

Instinctively, I catch it, but I'm flustered when the "dogs" come bounding after it.

Rarrr Rarrr Rarrr Rarrr.

"Just throw it!" shouts Joe. "As far as you can, so they get a good run!"

I hesitate, and the "dogs" press closer. When the spotted one jumps up, grazing my chest with a paw, it's enough to make me panic and pitch the stick with a sudden burst of strength. It spins across the field, taking the pack of "dogs" with it, and the stress they make me feel.

But the relief doesn't last long. Seconds later, the spotted "dog" hurtles back through the grass with the stick in its mouth, heading straight for me.

"Thank him and do it again!" says Joe. "Tell him what a good boy he is and give him another throw!"

Taking a slobbered-on piece of wood from the mouth of a drooling monster and possible killer of *real* dogs is the last thing I want to do right now. I know I should play along, but I flinch when the beast pushes the stick at me. I turn away, and he follows, persistent.

"Just do it! Just throw it!" Joe laughs. "He won't hurt you, I promise!"

As I turn away again, the other "dogs" barrel up and hurl themselves at me, leaping with jaws open to seize the stick. I let it go as I fall under the weight of them, unable to stop from toppling into the grass.

My heart hammers, and I'm short of breath when I hit. It's like something out of a nightmare as the pack of "dogs" converge around me, all fur and teeth and lolling pink tongues.

It only gets worse from there. One "dog" licks my face, dragging its tongue over my cheek, and I want to scream. Then another licks my face as well, and another.

And another. Stubby, the pointy-eared, short-legged one, licks my face with as much enthusiasm as he licked my jerky-scented fingers earlier.

I close my eyes, toss my head, and thrash on the ground, but it doesn't seem to help. The licking continues, three and four tongues at a time slathering my cheeks and nose and ears and mouth.

And then the *truly* unexpected happens. Against my will, against my better judgment, I start to *giggle*. Something about the combined action of those tongues on my face makes me squirm and laugh uncontrollably.

I reach up to bat away the monsters, and my hands come in contact with fur. I want to pull away, but I'm surprised at the feel of it; I've always been taught it's rough and prickly, but it's not. Something about it makes me want to keep touching it, running my hand over it just to feel the smooth texture.

"Are you okay?" Joe's standing over me, holding the fetch stick.

"This fur." I run my hands over Stubby's shaggy white-and-tan coat. "It isn't *soft* at all."

"Sure it is. It's *very* soft."

"*Soft* means it hurts my hands." I pet the "dog" some more, amazed. "This is the *opposite* of soft."

Joe nods and smiles. Maybe he understands. "Whatever you want to call it, 'Neath."

I frown up at him, still petting the monster. "My name is Beneathy."

"Well, now you have a nickname," says Joe. "I like 'Neath better, don't you?"

Just then, something crashes through the grass across the field, and Stubby yaps and scampers off. Joe quickly helps me up, and we look toward the commotion.

Five camouflage-wearing men riding "horses" are coming our way, looking grim. The "dogs" dart among them, tails wagging, calling out.

Rarrr Rarrr Rarrr.

"Hi, Mike!" Joe waves. "How was the hunt this time?"

The man at the front of the group—a broad-shouldered, middle-aged man with curly black hair and a bushy beard—just scowls and points at me. "Who the hell is that?"

"A new friend," says Joe. "His name is—"

Suddenly, a loud, blaring noise erupts from beyond the field, a single squawk like the blast of some kind of horn. Everyone looks in the direction of the sound, which is also the direction of camp.

Without another word, Mike kicks the sides of his "horse," and it bolts off toward camp at a fast gallop. The other four riders and "horses" follow just as fast, whipping past us with a flurry of "dogs" in their wake.

Joe sprints after them full-tilt, and I run beside him. "What's happening? What was that sound?"

"Grampa was calling for help," says Joe. "Camp is under attack."

———

As Joe and I race into camp on foot, the battle is already underway. The "horse"-riding hunters fire away with pistols and rifles, the woods booming with shot after shot.

All of which bounce off the gleaming white armor of the Nylon Knights without leaving a mark.

The Knights' weapons are much more effective. I see a male Knight spear a hunter's chest with a long white lance, driving its sharp point through his ribs and out his back, soaked with crimson. Another Knight's great green horse unfolds a spiny foreleg and swings it out to clamp the throat of a hunter, unleashing gushers of blood.

"Grampa!" Joe runs for the cabin, dodging Knights' horses and hunters' "horses" all around. Stubby scurries after him, too low to the ground to go very fast—or get out of the way of the hunter and wounded "horse" that suddenly topple toward him.

Without thinking, I dash over, grab Stubby by the scruff of his neck, and dive out from under the hunter and "horse." They slam down hard, just missing us as we roll under the wooden trough where Joe's "horse" drank water earlier.

Stubby whines as I keep him tucked under my arm and watch the battle rage from our hiding place. I feel his muscles twitch, but I don't let go. Maybe he wants to run to Joe, but I don't think he'll last long in the midst of that fight.

Not that the hunters are much of a match for the Knights. Soon, only two men in camouflage ride the battlefield amid the seven pristine Knights in white armor.

Suddenly, though, another player joins the fray. "Bastards!" From the doorway of the cabin, Grampa blasts away with a shotgun. "Rot in Hell!"

One of his shots hits a horse in its bulging green eye, and its head explodes. The horse goes down hard, throwing its rider to the ground without his lance.

Grampa's next shot isn't as lucky. It goes right between the pair of Knights who charge him with lances aimed directly at his chest.

They penetrate his chest from either side. Grampa drops the shotgun, and his eyes roll up in his head. He dangles like a meat puppet from the lances, held erect only by their crimson-dripping points.

Meanwhile, the pack of "dogs" attacks the Knight who lost his horse, lunging and snapping furiously. Their teeth have no chance of piercing the white armor, but they keep him pinned down, flailing at them with his barb-knuckled gauntlets.

He doesn't stay down for long, though. Just as one of the "dogs" pounces, knocking him over on his back, a winged figure bursts from the woods, heading straight for them and making a familiar sound.

K-klak klik buzzzz klak klik.

"Wazoo!" My heart jumps with excitement at the sound and sight of him—the realization that he isn't dead after all. He was only wounded and managed to recover from his injuries in time to come to the rescue.

K-klak klik buzzzz klak klik.

Swooping down at the "dogs," Wazoo unleashes black gas from one of his nozzles. Plumes of it swirl around the monsters, making them cough and retch and stagger off with their tails between their legs.

The Knight coughs, too, but he doesn't let it stop him from clambering to his feet and running back to help his comrades.

At this point, the outcome of the battle is no longer in doubt. The Knights surround the last two hunters, whose guns have stopped working. It won't be long until the circle of lances pointing at them moves inward, ending the fight.

In other words, I'm about to be rescued.

So why do I stay hidden under the trough? Wazoo buzzes around camp, spraying monsters with more of his black gas. I should be running to him.

But I'm not.

Stubby's body is warm against me. His fur feels good between my fingers. Something about him makes me want to hold on to him.

But my loyal dog, my precious Wazoo, is *right there*, awaiting what will surely be a joyous reunion with me. I can just imagine how wonderful it will feel to have his needles pierce my nose again, to smell his voice in my mind after so long apart.

So why am I thinking about sneaking away from him, crawling off into the forest with Stubby? Has this monster cast a spell on me?

I look at Stubby, and he looks back at me with wide, green eyes. For reasons unknown, he leans toward me and licks my nose with his wet, pink tongue.

For reasons unknown, I let him.

K-klak klik buzzzz klak klik.

Then, I watch Wazoo flying past, and I realize something.

I don't want to give up *either* of them. Perhaps, there's a way I won't have to.

PEOPLE SAY WINNING ISN'T EVERYTHING. BUT RIGHT NOW, IT'S all I can think about.

A few days ago, hiding under a trough at the hunters' camp in the woods, I wasn't sure what the future would bring. Now here I am, standing in front of thousands of people in Beastbless Stadium, waiting to hear if my greatest dream is about to come true.

Dozens of other Playtimers and their pets are lined up beside me on the artificial turf field, likewise waiting for the verdict. Do any of them want this as much as I do? It doesn't seem possible.

But winning *does*. The pet I have at my side is so wonderful in *every* way. He did so magnificently well in every event, I can't imagine him *not* winning.

But if he doesn't, it won't be the end of the world. What I went through at the camp prepared me for any adversity—even as it increased my chances of winning. *Our* chances.

"And now, the moment we've all been waiting for!" The female announcer's voice booms through the stadium P.A. system, drowning out the excited chatter from the stands. "The naming of the *grand prize* in this year's fabulous *Pet Pageant!*"

I take a deep breath to steady my nerves. Incompleta, who's sitting down in front, blows me a kiss for luck. Lovebite, who eventually came back to her that day in the woods, twines her segmented scarlet body around her head and neck, antennae twitching.

A drumroll begins as the announcer keeps talking. "This year's *Doggiest Dogaroonie* is…."

The tension in the stadium reaches its absolute peak…but I suddenly feel calm. Closing my eyes, I whisper my pet's name.

And then the announcer says it, too. "…*Wazoo!*"

The crowd roars and cheers. The other pet owners on the field slump with disappointment.

As for me, I turn to my dog and pat him on his furry head,

right between his pointy little ears. "Good boy, Wazoo! You did it!"

Wazoo's bristly proboscis twitches. He fidgets, unable to take a victory flight to mark the occasion.

That's because Stubby's white-and-tan fur, which is clipped to his body, keeps him from deploying his wings.

It's a small price to pay, though. I'm convinced that fur is what clinched Wazoo's winning the prize today. It made him unique, the best of both worlds—dog and monster, united.

Because of that fur, I am able to walk the perimeter of the field proudly with Wazoo and Stubby both by my side, in their own ways. And as we finish that victory lap and climb the Hill of Buddies in the middle of the field—all those hundreds of bodies processed during Playtime throughout the year, including the hunters and Grampa and Joe from the camp—I feel like I owe Wazoo and Stubby a debt of gratitude I can never truly repay.

So when I stand atop that hill, and the crowd continues to roar around me like the ocean, I give those two dogs—one real and one fake—the best tribute I can think of. I raise my arms overhead and cry out in the only languages they might appreciate.

Rarrr Rarrr Rarrr Rarrr.

K-klak klik buzzzz klak klik.

Though the meaning of what I've just said is forever lost to me, not that it truly matters or ever will.

ROBIN BRANDE

Robin Brande, besides being a prolific bestselling writer and a lawyer, is also a wilderness medic who understands a great deal about how tragic the outdoors can be.

This story is an amazing story that clearly uses the knowledge of nature. And takes it to a place right from the start that you will not expect.

You can get a lot more of Robin's wonderful stories in numbers of genres at https://www.robinbrande.com/

THE CANYON

ROBIN BRANDE

You want to know how it happened. Everybody does.

How I got this gift. How I got this power.

I don't think of it that way.

But you can decide.

My mother was an anthropologist. Dr. Susan Stringer. She was a university professor. Very smart. Funny, sweet, a great mom.

It was just the two of us. My biological father wasn't in the picture. The two of them met at a conference and had a one-night stand, and that was me.

We'd lived a few different places, wherever she was teaching. Missoula, Montana for a while when I really little, then University of Idaho later, and when she had a little trouble there we moved to Utah.

She got a job at SUU. Southern Utah University in Cedar City. Close to Cedar Breaks National Park.

There were a lot of beautiful places around there. We'd drive all over. Go camping and hiking. We loved Zion and Bryce and all the canyons all around. The hoodoos and spires and cliffs. My mother used to say it was like living inside a photograph, it was so unreal. Or like someone had painted us into a picture.

She studied ancient civilizations. Not like Greece and Rome, but places in South America and Africa and Asia. She studied artifacts and oral histories and petroglyphs.

Her main field was rituals. She was obsessed with them. Any old and weird thing some tribe used to do, she'd find out everything she could from every source she could find.

We never had much money. She couldn't travel the way she wanted. Some of her colleagues went all over the world looking at archeological digs or visiting museums or talking with other scholars, but my mom had me and she didn't think it was safe to take me any of those places. So she had to research it all from where we were.

We'd go camping somewhere and at night if we could make a fire she'd sit and tell me stories just like we were ancient people and she was a shaman or the storyteller and I was the rest of the tribe.

She wasn't my mom then, she was a leader. My guide. She was telling me things about life and the universe and holy things about the spirit. I could barely breathe sometimes, I was so mesmerized. She was wonderful.

Then on one of our campouts she started telling me a new kind of story.

About how nature is always the same. Societies change,

civilizations come and go, but nature—nature is always what it was.

If someone could do something in nature a thousand years ago, nature would let us do that same thing now.

She said it was like being able to see molecules under a microscope. Molecules existed always, but we just couldn't see them until we had the right instruments.

Or like light on a spectrum. Now we know about infrared and other light waves, but they existed always, whether or not we had the scientific ability to see them.

I nodded. I understood.

"Nature doesn't change," she said. "We just don't see sometimes. Or we forget something we already knew."

There were people in South America, she said, long ago, who knew how to make their dreams true.

There were tribes in Africa who had rituals to bring their dreams to life.

"Nature doesn't change," she kept saying. "People do. People forget."

She shined her headlight on a book she brought. Why she didn't show it to me in the daylight, I don't know. Why she waited to tell me all of this on the campout instead of back at our house, also don't know. She didn't usually hide things from me. It was just the two of us. We were best friends.

"I think this is true, Marnie," she said. She shined her headlight on a picture in the book. There were six people, brown skinned, sitting in a circle around a fire. They all had their eyes closed. Above them, coming out of their heads, were these kind of hazy images of those same people, but doing other things.

One wore an elaborate headdress.

"He dreams of being the chief," my mother said.

Another held a baby. Self-explanatory.

One wore a beak on a string tied over his nose, and he had long feathers growing out of his shoulders. The man having that thought sat cross-legged near the fire, but the flying version of him was taking off into the sky.

My mother pulled out another book. I didn't know about any of this. It was like she'd been planning how to tell me. It made me really nervous. I thought we were always honest, but it was like she'd had this secret, and I didn't know for how long.

In the second book there were only three people sitting beside a fire, and there was snow on the ground around them.

Above them, these amazing, beautiful swirls of light. Bright green, purple.

"What is that?" I asked.

"The Aurora Borealis," she said. "The Northern Lights.

Those are real. They still exist in northern climates. We could go see them this winter if we wanted."

I didn't know then. I thought we were just talking.

She said that book had the most information out of all of them. It had been written in the 1800s.

"Modern times," she said. That was modern to her. "I think we should go there," she said.

"Where?"

"Alaska." She pointed to the book. "This village where they did it still exists."

Like I said, we didn't have a lot of money. She had to borrow from one of her colleagues. Two tickets from Utah to Alaska, and then the cost of getting to that village, then their charge for the Northern Lights Experience.

We went over both our winter break. Left a few days after Christmas. We didn't buy each other any gifts. All the money was for the trip.

"We'll spend New Year's under the Northern Lights," my mother said. "It will be unforgettable."

I'd never traveled much, except when we moved or when we went on car trips. I'd never flown on a plane. It was thrilling and scary. But I loved it. I felt like I was four, not sixteen. Everything was so exciting. Even the snack cart.

It was cold, of course. But we'd packed everything warm. We took a second plane, much smaller, a lot scarier, to get closer to the village. Then a van picked us up and took us there.

It was a cute place. Really nice cabins, a nice lodge where you could sit by a fire with fur blankets over you while you drank hot chocolate. I played cards with some other kids who were there with their families. It was fun.

You could just stay there the whole time, or you could pay more to get a snow mobile to take you further out into the wilderness where there were no lights anywhere, just the lights from the sky. They gave you lots of fur blankets, a thermos of hot chocolate or coffee if you wanted, another thermos with soup, some bread and other snacks, and then they'd leave you for a while and come back and pick you up.

We did that. That was my mother's plan all along. To be left alone out there, under the lights, so she could try her ritual.

She didn't tell me about that. Not ahead of time. I thought we were just there to see the lights.

But once the snowmobiles dropped us off and the people from the lodge said they'd be back in two hours, my mother got us both warm and cozy on our camp chairs and covered in furs, and then she pulled out her book.

Her own book. One she'd been writing, without telling me.

A book filled with rituals about dreams.

Rituals from South America and Africa and Asia, some from Australia.

And ones from tribes in Alaska, involving the Aurora Borealis.

She started with that ritual first. It made the most sense. She spoke words, she made movements, I have to be honest, she scared me.

She wasn't like herself. She was… intense. Intense in a way I had never seen.

She shouted and sang and moved for two hours.

I shivered beneath the furs and watched her.

She started crying after a while. "It doesn't work! Why doesn't it work for me?"

I didn't say anything. I'm not sure she even remembered I was there.

The snowmobiles came back and picked us up. My mother was so depressed.

The next morning she paid for a second night.

"I'll try one of the others," she told me. "Don't give up, Marnie."

I wasn't giving up. I wasn't involved at all. I was like a stuffed animal, just sitting with her while she did it. She didn't talk to me or ask me any questions or ask me for any help.

It was New Year's night. The first night of a new year. My mother sang and hopped around in the snow and waved her arms and shouted words.

I drank cocoa this time because I was cold. And I wanted some comfort. My mother was acting so strange.

But it didn't work. My mother cried again. It was starting to feel like a cycle.

Her excitement, her ideas about how to make it happen this time, then trying, then failing, crying, depressed.

We went out again. And again. We couldn't afford it, but she kept paying.

We had to book extra nights at our cabin too, because she hadn't planned on staying there that long. She thought she would succeed the first night. We had to change our flight back too.

Then finally, January fourth.

The South American chant.

Nothing to do with Aurora Borealis, but it was the right ritual after all.

I won't tell you what it was. You'll try it. I don't want anyone else to ever do it.

The sky. That's how we knew: the sky.

The lights all around us were purple and pink and red. Swirling in giant round waves. So beautiful. So unearthly.

And then my mother said the right words. She moved her arms in just the right way. She sang her song in exactly the right pitch.

The sky became white.

Not swirling anymore, but long fingers reaching down from the heavens, white spears of it, pushing toward the ground, pushing into both of us.

Punching into my chest.

Throwing my mother off her feet into the snow.

It hurt. But it felt glorious. Like something alien entering my body and making me suddenly feel alive. Like I'd been asleep for sixteen years. Now I could see and smell and feel. I could hear everything: the stars, the white light, my mother's heartbeat. The heartbeat of the whole world.

I felt overjoyed. I leapt from my chair onto my feet and started jumping up and down.

My mother was laughing and shouting and crying.

She ran over to me and hugged me. We both jumped up and down together. We were laughing and screaming. I've never felt happier in my life.

"Do something!" my mother shouted. "Come on, Marnie!"

I started running. It felt so natural and wonderful.

Like in a dream.

And like in a dream, the faster I ran, I wanted to go faster still. I ran faster than I ever had in my life.

And it felt natural to stretch out my arms.

And then to move them. Up and down.

And my feet lifted off the snow.

Just like in a dream.

I was dreaming. I'd swear it. Nothing felt the slightest bit real. I soared over my mother's head and could see her gazing up at me, so happy, amazed, happier than I'd ever seen her.

I felt perfect. For a while. Maybe five whole minutes. Then it was like I woke up. Realized this was true.

Panicked.

I started twisting up there in the air. I lost my way. My arms weren't working right anymore. My body felt so heavy and wrong.

I could hear my mother screaming. I was falling so fast toward the snow. She screamed and ran to where I was falling.

But I landed perfectly on my feet.

She stared at me, shocked.

"Marnie."

"Mom." I ran to her and held on to her and both of us cried for a while.

The snowmobiles came back.

We had to act like nothing had happened.

When I hugged her I could feel something different about my mother.

Something warm in the center of her chest.

The next day we paid for the snowmobiles one more time and went out for our final night.

"Try it," my mother said. Even before she did the ritual again.

I felt nervous. Afraid. But also curious and excited.

I ran. Flapped my arms. And lifted off the snow.

My mother tried it. But it didn't work for her.

She tried other things: hopping, running faster, flapping her arms faster—nothing worked.

She was devastated. All that effort, and it had only worked for me.

She did the entire ritual again. Maybe that was the problem. Maybe it only worked for one person at a time.

The lights were green that night, but then they turned white again. The same piercing shards pushing down from the sky.

Into her heart, into mine.

I didn't feel so happy this time.

Just… anxious.

I threw off the fur blankets and started running again. I took off into the sky. I flew like I needed it. Because I did. Flapped hard and then started swimming in the air, my arms pulling me forward like I was swimming against a current.

My mother knelt in the snow and sobbed.

But I had to keep flying. I couldn't come down and console her.

I could see the snowmobiles from the distance and knew I'd have to come back down.

But it made me so angry. I didn't want to have to stop.

But my mother was in bad shape. I knew I needed to help her.

So I flew until the last possible moment, then came down and helped her get under control.

And that was the last time any part of my life felt normal.

We left Alaska. I was a shaking, jittery mess. I couldn't sit still anymore. I couldn't focus on anything. She'd be talking to me and in my head I was saying shut up, shut up, shut up, because all I could think about anymore was whether I would ever get to fly again.

It was like someone had infected me with this horrible, insatiable desire. Like those people you read about who scratch their skin off, they can't ever satisfy their itch.

At night I started flying. All night. I'd leave our house as soon as it was dark, and fly for the next twelve hours.

By morning I was exhausted. I couldn't go to school. My mother wasn't speaking to me. She was so distraught that it hadn't worked for her.

And then everything changed again.

One morning I came back from flying and she was up waiting for me in the kitchen.

Ecstatic. So excited.

"I had a dream last night," she said. "One of those falling dreams where you wake up right before you hit the ground."

I waited to hear the rest. I didn't have a good feeling.

"You've had flying dreams since you were a little girl," my mother said. "You always told me."

I could see where this was going. "No, Mom."

"Yes," she said. "We have to try."

She cancelled her classes for the day and we drove to Cedar Breaks.

I begged her not to do it.

It was insane. I begged her not to try.

But she was as jittery as I was, ever since the ritual worked.

I could work out some of that by flying all night long.

She had no place to get rid of the feeling.

There were dark circles under her eyes. She looked exhausted and sick. She kept saying, "Yes, it will work, it worked for you," and I kept telling her no, and then she shouted, "MARNIE! I GET TO HAVE IT TOO!"

And she jumped.

Over the edge of a cliff.

I screamed. I jumped after her, flying, knowing it would be impossible to save her.

I was too weak. I couldn't catch her or carry her. I couldn't carry anything and still flap my arms.

My mother screamed, screamed with joy. As she fell fast down the face of the cliff.

And when she was near the bottom, about to die—

Her body suddenly stopped in midair.

Just like in a dream.

Suspended like she was held up by cables.

Perfectly horizontal, a smooth stop.

I hovered beside her.

My mother laughed.

I laughed too, out of relief.

But it was crazy. I could see that. Much crazier than being able to fly.

"I want to try it again," my mother said.

I didn't argue. I understood what that feeling was like.

Using my arms to keep me up, I pushed her body with my feet. Got her to a place on the side of the cliff where there were places to put her hands and feet so she could climb down the rest of the way.

She was only a few feet from the bottom. It didn't take her long.

We realized there were no trails where we were. It took us the rest of the day to climb out.

I could have flown, easily, but I stayed with my mother. For safety.

Because any time we got high enough out, she would turn around and jump again.

I made her stop falling all the way to the bottom. "We have to get out before dark." So she only fell halfway sometimes, or a quarter, but I couldn't make her stop falling all together.

She'd jump, I'd fly down to her, then push her to the side so she could climb.

It was past dark when we finally made it to the top.

I was worried she'd jump again.

She wasn't thinking clearly anymore. It was like a drug. It took hold.

I held onto her tight and got her into the car. I was afraid to let her drive. I thought she might drive the car off a cliff, so even though I was new to it, I drove.

That night her eyes looked glassy. And she had the biggest smile on her face. She was giddy. Couldn't stop talking. How wonderful it all was, how it felt.

I was exhausted after the day, but I still had needs of my own. I didn't fly as long that night, but I still flew.

And in the morning my mother cancelled her classes again.

This was our life now.

I stopped going to school too. Not because of flying, but to keep my mother safe.

I told people she was home schooling me. She told the university she was sick and needed a leave of absence.

We were almost out of money.

Every day she had to jump.

"Mom, one of us needs to work."

"I know," she said. She tapped her hand against the kitchen table, so much energy she couldn't contain it.

"What are we going to do?" I asked.

"I'll get a loan," she said.

She did, somehow. That bought us another few months.

But by the summer we were behind on our rent and I had to get a job. I started working at a place that served only breakfast and lunch. I didn't make much, but it was something. And I was always free by late afternoon.

My mother and I made a deal. We looked at the maps together and decided the places she could go. We'd been exploring the canyons and knew which ones she could climb out of on her own. She had to fall to a specific spot, but then there were rocks close enough that she could grab and pull herself over to the side.

And I would always fly down there after my shift was over in the afternoon and push her if she was stuck somewhere.

But my mother was a sneak.

No, not my mother, the condition.

Ever since she found out about the ritual, it's like she locked me out.

She lied. More than I realized.

About why we were going to Alaska. About what she was going to do there.

And now, about the jumping.

I came home one afternoon to change into my flying clothes, and there was a note.

Change of plans.

That's all it said.

We had gone over the map the night before. One of her regular routes. No problem.

Change of plans.

My blood froze.

My mother had been acting more and more erratic.

More obsessed.

Taking, I warned her, too many risks.

"But it feels so good," she said with a smile. "The falling. You don't know what it's like."

"I do know, Mom—"

"You don't!" she snapped. "You don't," she said more softly. "I hate always having to climb back up. I just wish I could fall a thousand miles."

Change of plans.

It was like a drug. I knew it. I've felt it in myself. Like something inside your veins. Or invading your brain. Something you can't logic yourself out of.

It doesn't matter if you know it's dangerous. It doesn't

matter if you have a daughter. If you lose your job. If you lose your house.

You need it. You have to have it all the time. Nothing matters but how wonderful it makes you feel.

The car was gone. She always took it. I knew the way to fly to go meet her in the spots where she always went.

She wasn't in any of them.

The car wasn't there.

I flew from canyon to canyon. Cliff after cliff. Already knowing she wasn't there, but I had to look.

When it was dark, I kept looking, calling out for her, screaming.

"MOM! MOTHER! ARE YOU HERE?"

Calling for her until I lost my voice.

So tired of flying I was afraid my arms would give up.

Some time in the early hours I had to rest for a while. It was cold, even in the summer. I wasn't dressed warmly enough. I hunkered in an overhang just to get out of the wind. I slept, badly.

My mother could be suspended somewhere in midair.

No food or water. Cold.

Maybe calling for me, afraid.

In the morning I searched again. I never found her car.

I went home and looked at more maps.

Over the next several days I went to Zion, Escalante, and Bryce. We had talked about camping in those places later in the summer to give her some new places to jump.

I never found her car.

I never found her.

I could see her in my mind's eye, unconscious from lack of

water. Lying horizontal near the bottom of some deep, deep canyon where no one would ever find her.

How long did it take her to realize she'd made a terrible mistake?

That I wouldn't know where to look for her, and couldn't help her over to the side?

When the giddiness had worn off, when she'd fallen further than ever before, when that drug flooded her veins for a while, but then the drug was starting to leave—

Did she call for me?

Not on a phone, there was no signal in the canyons. We had experimented with that before.

Called out for me as a mother for her daughter, "MARNIE! HELP ME!"

Did she call until she was hoarse?

Did she fall asleep that first night still believing I would come and save her?

Or did she fall asleep knowing she would die there and I'd never find her no matter how long I searched?

I did search. For weeks. Knowing she was dead now, but still wanting to find her body.

I stopped working. Let the landlord lock us out. Lock me out. I was alone now. I knew it, but I didn't want to think it.

I turned seventeen in August.

I still searched until the end of September.

I started over. Moved to a new town. Got a new job. Lied about my age. Lied about my name. Lied about everything.

I stopped looking for her. I didn't want to find whatever her body might look like now, picked apart by scavenging animals.

Why had my mother done it? Not the falling—I understand that. It's a compulsion. She couldn't help it. It would be like asking a person not to swallow or blink.

But why did she have to take us to Alaska? Why did she have to do the ritual?

Weren't we happy as we were?

We read books to each other aloud at night, snuggled together on the couch.

We cooked together. We watched movies. We went hiking and camping. I told her everything. I didn't need other friends, I had her.

She didn't need other friends, she had me.

I was smart once. I did well in school. I was the biological daughter of two smart professors. I was going to college. Maybe major in geography. Or anthropology, to follow after my mother.

I did follow after my mother.

But it didn't matter.

I never found her.

So tell me now.

Is this a gift? Is it a power?

Or is it a condition. A compulsion.

Imagine you can save a life, but it means you have to save every life. All the time, night and day, good people and bad, every single person until you're too exhausted to live anymore.

Pretend you can read minds. But every mind. The sick ones too, the ones you wouldn't want to spend even a split second inside, but you have no control, you have to hear and see every revolting idea that passes through some sadistic, violent person's head. You can't block it out. You have to accept it.

But you're so lucky. It's your gift.

But I know you don't see. You don't believe me. I can tell by the look in your eyes.

You're just like everybody else. In your head right now you're saying, "But…"

You still want it. I know.

You'll think about my story and you'll pick out certain details.

What book did she say her mother read? Which ritual did she use? Where was the village with the Aurora Borealis?

You'll think about what my mother said. That nature is always the same. That if we could do something a thousand years ago, we can still do it now.

But some things—some things we shouldn't.

Think about that. Think about it when you're falling or

flying or stuck in your endless dream. Think about how hard I tried to warn you.

It's true, just like my mother said. Nature doesn't change, it's just that people forget.

But she didn't understand that's the point.

Some things are meant to be forgotten.

But I've got to go now.

I have to fly.

O'NEIL DE NOUX

O'Neil De Noux takes his amazing skills as one of the best writers of detective fiction working today and gives us another wonderful trip into the past. 1891 New Orleans to be exact. The places and events and characters just come alive in O'Neil's powerful hands.

O'Neil has published about fifty novels with more coming regularly. His awards include The United Kingdom Short Story Prize, the Shamus Award (for best private eye fiction), the Derringer Award (for excellence in mystery short fiction) and Police Book of the Year.

Two of his stories have appeared in the prestigious Best American Mystery Stories annual anthology and I noticed he had another in the recommended reading for this last year's volume. He won the Shamus for a story in 2020. You can find out a lot more about his work at his website http://www.oneildenoux.com/

MARIA'S HAND

O'NEIL DE NOUX

Monday, 15 June 1891

The man on the beat was waiting for Dugas at the Tenth Precinct station house with the trunk with the woman's hand inside.

"Ah, you must be our detective," the patrolman said as Dugas stepped from the police boat to the station house dock, "I'm Donahoe. Joe Donahoe." The big man extended his hand to shake which Dugas missed and fell back on the boat, twisting his left ankle as his leg hit a guide rail. He winced and climbed off without assistance, his ankle burning now.

Patrolman Donahoe was pushing forty and burly with thick sandy hair and a matching moustache, along with a reddish drinker's nose. He'd left his sky blue bowler inside the station, his sky blue New Orleans police shirt streaked with sweat as he wiped his brow with a gray handkerchief.

"Come on in." Donahoe turned and went into the new

wood-frame station house built along the New Basin Canal for the ten patrolmen responsible for the thinly-settled district at the rear of the city which ran all the way to Lake Pontchartrain.

Detective Jacques Dugas—six feet tall, one hundred eighty pounds with dark brown eyes, wore his dark brown hair parted down the middle and his moustache neatly trimmed. Twenty-six years old, he was young for a detective. A French-American, he was one of the few non-Irishmen on the job. Today he wore a lightweight blue suit.

A elderly man with a thick shock of gray hair, a matching unkempt beard and skin so dark it looked blue-black, sat on a bench across from the desk sergeant's high counter. Wearing a long coat over several layers of shirts, well-worn dungarees and work boots, it was obvious the old man was living rough on the down-and-out.

Donahoe led the way around the counter to a desk, Dugas limping slightly. The trunk was a brown portmanteau, nearly three feet long, two feet high, with a thick handle atop between two snap-locks which had been forced open.

"Look inside," Donahoe said, folding his arms.

Dugas peeked in and saw the hand resting atop a pile of clothes. It didn't look real, more like a manikin's, whitish-pink in color, long nails painted bright red. It was a left hand, a thin wedding band on its ring finger; the hand had been severed just above the wrist in what looked like one neat cut.

"Fella over there brought it in after breaking open the locks," Donahoe's voice had the typical copper's accusatory tone, "claims he found it on the side of the road."

Dugas looked at the elderly man, "What's your name?"

"Homer Jones, suh."

"What road?" Dugas gingerly moved around the counter.

"Bayou Road, suh." The man staring at his limp.

Dugas took out his note pad and pencil as he sat on the bench next to Homer. He'd already written the date and time he'd received the call and quickly jotted his time of arrival, glancing up at the clock on the wall, seeing it was nine-ten a.m., then wrote Donahoe's name and the name Homer Jones.

He jotted 'Bayou Road' and then asked, "When did you find it?"

"This mornin' just after sunup. It was 'tween the road and the bayou like someone just 'trew and missed the water. I tried not to break the locks. But I could feel somethin' inside…"

And he wanted what was inside. Homer looked Dugas in the eyes with such sincerity, the way an innocent man looked a cop straight in the eyes, nothing to hide. He answered the next questions without hesitation. He'd seen no one in the area this morning. He lived in a shack, as he called it, up the road a ways closer to the lake. He was headed to mooch a hand-out from one of the kitchens along the 'back a town'— indicating the Faubourg St. John and the new residential Faubourg Pontchartrain being built on the marshy area between the city and the lake.

"I seen it had women's clothes and shoes. The hand was at the bottom and I didn't think it was real 'til I touch it. So I closed up the trunk and went lookin' for a copper. Didn't want to just leave the trunk there with a lady's hand inside."

"I searched him," said Donahoe. "Don't look like he stole anything from the trunk." A disapproving smirk on the copper's face now as Donahoe added, "He's just one of them bums camped up the bayou across from the park. We're in the process of rousting them for the developers."

Dugas to Homer, "Anyone you know lives near where you found the trunk?"

"No, suh. Most of our shacks are up the bayou."

Rubbing his ankle, Dugas closed his eyes and distracted himself with a vision of semi-rural Bayou Road, the oldest road in the entire area, an old Indian trail running alongside Bayou St. John, predating even the French.

"I intend to ask around," Homer said. "Maybe somebody seen somethin' and I can let you know."

Donahoe injected, "We don't need no bums investigatin' anything."

Dugas stood, nodding to Homer, before asking Donahoe, "You finished with him?"

"I guess so."

Leading Homer Jones outside, Dugas stopped him and leaned against the rail surrounding the low porch of the station. They had their backs to the station so Donahoe couldn't hear. Dugas kept his voice low as he handed Homer one of the new business cards his captain had distributed to all the detectives. "This has my name and how to get a hold of me. You can read, can't you?"

"Yes, suh. Mister Detective Dugas." Homer looking at the card now.

"I want you to do just as you suggested," Dugas said, reaching down to massage his ankle which was tightening up badly. "Ask around. People will talk to you when they won't talk to me."

"I know that. I seen a lot myself bein' around the old plantation all my life."

It took Dugas a second to realize, so he asked, "You used to work the Allard Plantation?" This large defunct plantation was now City Park, 1,500 acres just being developed into an urban park.

"Yes, suh. Born there in 1831. I was a field hand 'til the war came. Ran off and joined the Billy Yanks."

Dugas stared at the former slave who'd run off to join the U.S. Army during the Civil War. The old man's eyes got a troubled look in them. "I was wounded bad at the crater. Petersburg. June 30, 1864."

My God, thought Dugas, the Petersburg crater. Everyone knew the story, even Dugas who wasn't even born until after the war. Near the end of the war, during the siege of Petersburg, some enterprising army sappers had dug under the confederate lines and blew up an entire section of the breastworks, creating a huge crater. The Yankees sent in colored troops to swarm through the break in the line, only the crater was so deep and wide the rebels had time to recover before the troops could get out of the bowl, which became a shooting gallery.

"I tried to surrender," Homer said, as if following Dugas's thoughts. "But the Rebs would have none of that. Kept killin' everyone. I got shot three times and crawl out the back side and the Yankees pulled me clear. Lost all ma' friends that day. Every one of 'em."

Homer turned his brown eyes to Dugas. "Your Daddy fought in the war?"

Dugas shook his head. "I'm the first one in my family to

speak English. During the war we remained Frenchmen, not about to fight for the Rebels or Yankees."

"Smart folks."

When Dugas shook the old man's hand, he slipped him a dollar and Homer thanked him kindly and walked off down the New Basin Canal. Back inside the station house, Donahoe was sitting behind the counter.

"You got quite a mystery on your hands, Det. Dugas."

Dugas hobbled back to the trunk.

"Hurt your leg?"

Dugas nodded as he lifted the hand out to examine it closely. No other wounds were visible and nothing beneath the fingernails. Victims often scratch their assailants, leaving skin under the nails. These were clean. He gently placed it on the table and pulled out the clothes, one piece at a time.

The skirt was linen with a matching jacket. The shoes were labeled "Made in NYC" and were size four. He found a laundry mark on a cream colored silk blouse that read: EKD LAUN.

"Think he cut it off when she was still alive?" Donahoe sat with his hands behind his head.

"Most likely post-mortem."

"Huh?"

"Few people would let someone cut their hand off without jerking. The wound's too neat."

Donahoe smiled for the first time but it wasn't a friendly one. "I heard 'a you. The Frenchie Detective. Everyone says you're pretty smart. You gonna need to be to solve this one." With that Donahoe picked up his bowler and walked out.

THE CORONER WAS 'FAIRLY' CONFIDENT THE DISMEMBERMENT was post-mortem. Dugas noted it in his notes, as well as the approximate time of dismemberment, within the last forty-eight hours and the approximate age of the victim, between twenty and thirty.

Leaving the portmanteau in the evidence locker at the Detective Bureau, Dugas took the blouse to the nearest laundry whose proprietor recognized the laundry mark and directed Dugas to the Edkins Laundry, adjacent to St. Louis #3 Cemetery on Esplanade Avenue.

Alighting slowly from the mule-drawn streetcar, Dugas stood with his weight on his right leg and looked across the avenue at Edkins Laundry, which occupied the bottom floor of a two-story wood frame house next to the white walls of the cemetery.

The owner-operator, a short squat man named Eldon

Edkins recognized the blouse as owned by one of his regular customers, Maria Alcamo. Dugas asked for an address.

"She's the wife of the baker right down the street," Edkins pointed down Esplanade. "It's called Pane Fresco. The bakery."

"When was the last time you saw Mrs. Alcamo?"

Edkins checked his book and said, "Last Tuesday, the ninth."

"Was she with someone?"

"Someone. No. She always comes alone. Is she is trouble?"

Dugas shook his head and asked, "What does she look like?"

"Pretty." The man's eyes lit up. "Very pretty with dark hair and dark eyes. Italian, you know. Sort of sultry."

"What does her husband look like?"

"Him, I've never seen."

Mr. Alcamo was a big man, a good three inches taller tan Dugas's six-feet, and balding, a thick man with large arms. Clean shaven, he had deep-set green eyes and greeted Dugas with a warm smile from behind the counter. Pane Fresco, which Dugas knew meant 'fresh bread' in Italian, smelled of freshly baked bread and cinnamon and other spices, nutmeg most likely.

The smile went away when Dugas opened the lapel of his coat to show his gold NOPD star-and-crescent badge, then held up the blouse. The big man's face went from surprise to confusion to fear, as the man asked, "What has happened?"

Dugas asked to see his wife.

The big man's chin sank. "She no live here anymore. She left me. Just before Christmas." He looked at the blouse again as Dugas placed it atop the glass counter. Through quivering lips, he said, "Por favore, senoré policia…is Maria OK?"

Dugas just stared into the deep set eyes as they filled with tears.

"No. No," the man cried as his shoulders slumped and he broke down. An older woman came scrambling out of the back as Alcamo lay his head on the counter and sobbed. In shrill Italian, too rapid for Dugas to follow, the woman was alternately trying to calm Alcamo and cursing Dugas, calling him a devil of dubious birth. Those phrases were easily iden-tified. The old woman spotted the blouse and went suddenly quiet.

It was then Dugas noticed another woman standing in the doorway leading to the back of the bakery. She looked like a smaller version of the baker but still had all of her black hair. Eyeing Dugas she said, "I am Louisa. Who are you?"

Like her brother, Louisa Alcamo spoke excellent English. As the big man struggled to control his sobbing, Dugas learned from Louisa that Maria Alcamo was living the 'high life' since leaving her husband. "She hangs out in saloons. I think she's whoring it." Which sent the husband into another long sobbing tirade, the old woman, who turned out to be the baker's mother, rubbed his back and telling him, in Italian, to let it out.

"Which saloons?" Dugas.

"Take your pick. She ain't picky."

None of the Alcamos, who lived above the bakery, knew where Maria lived now, neither did any of the neighbors. By the time Dugas returned to the bakery, Mr. Alessio Alcamo was more composed. Dugas took the big baker to the Central

Police Station to interview, getting him away from his mama and sister, getting him in a more controlled environment.

Before leaving, Dugas asked to look around the apartment and the bakery. If a body had been dismembered, they'd done a good job of cleaning up. The bakery and apartment were clean but not freshly scrubbed, which would have increased Dugas's suspicion.

"Do you have a picture of Maria I could borrow?"

Louisa brought a portrait of Maria to Dugas, telling him he could keep it. They had plenty as Maria was vain and had many pictures. It was a five by seven inch portrait of a very pretty young woman sitting in a chair. Maria's dark eyes stared right into the camera lens, her long hair pulled away from her lovely face with combs. Maria had a delicate nose and finely sculptured lips On second look, Dugas could see a mischievous glint in those dark eyes.

Turning the photo over Dugas was surprised no studio name was on back.

"Where did she have this picture taken?"

"Who knows?"

PERCHED ON THE SMALL WOODEN CHAIR IN THE TINY INTERVIEW room of the Detective Bureau, Alessio Alcamo brought none of the hysterics with him. Leaning his large arms on the little table and staring Dugas in the eye, he answered every question directly, without hesitation. Dugas studied the man, focusing on the way he answered rather than his blanket denials. Alcamo hadn't seen Maria since January, when she came back briefly to remove the belongings she'd left before Christmas. He had no idea where she was living. He rebuffed the advice of his mother, sister and friends to seek Maria out.

"If she want to go, I must let her go."

Sometimes a cop had to go with his gut feelings. The husband, especially an estranged husband, was the first suspect in a case like this. Dugas was careful not to mention they'd found a hand that was most likely Maria's, even when he showed the thin wedding band the coroner had removed from the hand.

Alcamo nodded, confirming it was Maria's wedding band, pointing to a slight bulge on one side where the band had worn down unevenly. Dugas told him the band would be returned to him once the case was resolved. Naturally, once Dugas was finished his initial questioning, Alcamo wanted to know what happened to Maria.

"We don't know exactly what happened," said Dugas explaining about the trunk with some of her clothes in it. He watched closely when he told Alcamo about the hand.

The big baker's face seemed frozen for a long minute before he focused newly shocked eyes at Dugas and said, "Oh, my God. Poor Maria." He made the sign of the cross and wiped a single tear that rolled down his face.

Alcamo did not recognize the trunk, which Dugas had examined closely, finding no markings or anything to indicate ownership. It didn't appear new. "I never seen this trunk before," said Alcamo, but he recognized all of the remaining clothes and shoes as his wife's.

Stepping out of the interview room, Dugas led Alcamo to his desk at the rear of the Bureau and had the big man sit in the wooden chair next to the worn wooden desk as Dugas put the finishing touches to the man's official statement.

"Read this over and sign at the bottom of each page."

As Alcamo read his three page statement, Dugas spotted the acting-commander of the Detective Bureau crossing the squad room with another detective. Lieutenant Ed O'Meara was forty-six, portly, standing five-six with red hair, a moustache and mutton chops along the sides of his wide face. His companion, named McCandless, also stood five-six with dark brown hair, a full moustache and was even thinner than Dugas and a couple years older.

"And who's this?" O'Meara pointed at Alcamo as he arrived. "This the husband?"

Dugas nodded.

"You a Wop?"

Alcamo nodded as Dugas passed him his fountain pen to sign the statement.

"A Moustache Pete sittin' right here," O'Meara turned to McCandless.

"He's not a Moustache Pete," Dugas said, nodding to Alcamo to keep signing. "He doesn't have a moustache, doesn't live in the Quarter, isn't a gangster. He owns his own business."

"The Quarter? You mean Little Palermo? He's Sicilian, ain't he?"

Alcamo nodded again as he signed the last page of his statement.

"There you go," O'Meara waved a hand. "Moustache Pete." He looked at McCandless for support and got nothing.

Dugas was surprised when McCandless sided with him. "If he ain't got a handlebar moustache, doesn't stand around leaning on lamp posts in the French Quarter eyeballing passersby, isn't an olive-skinned gangster, then he's just a plain Guinea."

O'Meara glared at McCandless, then turned his glare to Dugas. "What kinda business?"

"Bakery on Esplanade Avenue."

"Pane Fresco?" McCandless now.

"Si," Alcamo answered.

"I've been there. It's a good bakery, lieutenant. A very good one."

"What the hell do you know?" O'Meara grabbed Alcamo's left elbow and pulled the big man up. "I'm gonna sweat this Wop."

"I already did," Dugas said, his voice rising slightly as he pushed back his chair.

"I don't see no marks on him."

Dugas kept his voice firm and low, "We sweat them differently." He stood and leaned his hands on his desk. "You're not taking him. This is my case, lieutenant."

O'Meara was so surprised he let go of Alcamo's elbow, took a menacing step forward and growled, "I out rank you."

"I'm the case officer. You want us to take it up with the superintendent, then let's go. I think the Italian legation is still in town."

That caused O'Meara to pause. The feud between the Irish and Italians, which erupted last October when New Orleans's first police chief David Hennessey was gunned down. The situation exploded when the Sicilians accused of his murder were acquitted only to be lynched in the courtyard of parish prison by an angry mob before they could be released. Word on the street was some of the men lynched were, in fact, innocent. The Italian Government was still threatening war.

"Yeah," McCandless injected. "I heard that the U.S. might have to pay reparations."

O'Meara was dumb, but not that dumb. All they needed was another lynched Italian business man. He huffed at Dugas and tried another tack. "Me friend Donahoe tells me you were cuddling with a darkie what found this trunk."

"I've never cuddled with a man in my life. Sounds like something you Irish do."

This caused O'Meara's eyes to bulge and drew a grin from McCandless.

"Damn Creole," O'Meara stammered. "I ought to thrash you. You don't know how to treat Wops or darkies."

Creoles knew exactly how. Not much trouble between the French and Spanish Creoles and the free-men-of-color until the Kaintocks, as the first Americans were called, came down the Mississippi from Kentucky and points beyond.

"No need to get worked up, lieutenant," Dugas said. "My victim is Sicilian after all."

It wasn't much, but O'Meara took it as a face-saving gesture, stomping off with, "Yeah. Nothin' but a dead Wop."

Alessio Alcamo let out a long breath as the angry lieutenant retreated. Dugas just shrugged as McCandless said, "He's afraid of Captain Gray. Everyone knows you're Gray's fair-haired boy. Calls you 'the smart one.'" Gray, their no-nonsense captain, was Irish of course and sharp as a fencer's coil. Everyone, including O'Meara was aware his command was tenuous as well as temporary.

We'll see how smart I am with this case, thought Dugas as he began to lead Alcamo out. Turning, he called back to Mac, "Didn't mean to offend you with that Irish crack."

"You ain't all that smart after all, Mr. French Detective. McCandless is Scottish."

Tuesday, 16 June 1891

Early morning fog covered Bayou St. John completely, extending into the oaks of City Park. The squawk of blue jays and the lilting calls of mockingbirds echoed as Dugas walked up Bayou Road toward a group of shacks across the bayou from the park. His ankle was so tight he had trouble moving it and couldn't put his full weight on it.

He wore black boots today with his gray suit. A fire in a barrel in front of one shack drew Dugas who watched two men with tin cups in hand as they moved cautiously away from him. He was about to call out to them when a voice called out behind him.

"Mr. Detective Dugas!"

He turned to see Homer Jones come out of a particularly thick fog bank with another man. Homer smiled, "This here's John Racey," nodding to his companion. Each carried a tin cup and Dugas smelled coffee.

Stepping up, Homer added, "He seen something yesterday morning."

Racey was white, around fifty, about five-five and skinny with a mop of dirty brown hair on his pointy head, a beard and wore several layers of clothing. Looking down at his raggedy boots, Racey said, "I seen a wagon stop right where Homer found the trunk. Early morning yesterday." He looked up with bloodshot, drinker's eyes. "A man with blond hair was drivin' the wagon and I seen him climb down but I didn't see no trunk. Then he drove off in a hurry."

"Was he alone?"

"Yeah. It was a flatbed wagon with one seat, drawn by a mule."

"Could you identify the man if you saw him again?"

Racey shook his head. "I hid behind some bushes sos he won't bother me and seen him turn the wagon around drive away back up the road."

"Back toward Esplanade?"

"Yes, suh."

"Did he throw anything into the bayou?"

"No. I woulda heard a splash. He didn't go near the water."

Dugas turned to Homer who said he'd asked everyone he knew and Racey was the only one who saw anything. He showed them Maria's portrait and Homer was quite shaken.

"It was <u>her</u> hand?"

"We think so."

Homer shook his head and looked over at the park. "Such a pretty lady."

"You did well," Dugas said as he passed each man a dollar. "Mind if we ask around some more?"

"No, suh. Let's go talk."

They spoke with eleven other men along Bayou Road as the sun rose higher in the sky and the oaks across the bayou came out of the fog with their gray Spanish moss beards, like hulking ghosts, until the sunlight turned their dark leaves into sparkles of green.

None of the other men had seen anything. Dugas thanked Homer again as he walked back down Bayou Road toward Esplanade Avenue. Looking at the sluggish brown bayou, Dugas smelled the brackish water and remembered how this entire area was once a lawless swamp inhabited by thieves and desperate women who did anything to survive. He wondered where they'd gone, then figured their lifespan wasn't that long.

———

DUGAS FOUND DONAHOE SWINGING HIS BILLY CLUB AS HE strolled past Smith's Saloon just down Esplanade from the bayou.

"Boyo!" Donahoe called out. "Why you limping? One of them bums bit you on the leg?"

Dugas fought his anger, gritted his teeth instead and said, "Buy you a beer?"

"Is the Pope Catholic?" Donahoe wheeled and led the way into the saloon that smelled of cigar smoke and stale beer. Besides the bartender there were six men at three different tables. Donahoe sidled up to the bar, laid his billy atop and called out, "Barman, two mugs of your best brew."

"Make one a coffee," Dugas said, which drew the attention of two of the men who gave him a long look. Showing Maria's picture to Donahoe, Dugas explained who she was and about Pane Fresco just down the avenue.

"Don't know how I missed a looker like that," Donahoe said shaking his head before downing half his mug in one swallow.

The coffee was surprisingly good.

Dugas said, "A blond haired man riding a mule-drawn flat wagon stopped where the trunk was found early yesterday morning only a short time before Homer Jones came across the trunk. He may be our man."

Donahoe pulled the mug from his mouth, his brow furrowed now. "You don't say?" He took a small sip and looked at Dugas differently. "That's good work. I mean there's lotsa blond haired men, but we got somethin' to work with, don't we? And you identified her just from her hand. Maybe youse as smart as they say."

Finishing his beer the burly patrolman took Maria's picture to every table in the bar, had the two men with their hats on remove them, then asked if anyone knew her or a blond man who would have driven a mule-drawn wagon along Bayou Road yesterday morning. No one had.

Stepping back into the sunshine, Donahoe put his bowler back on his head and asked Dugas why he never wore a hat.

"Messes up my hair," Dugas said with a smirk.

Donahoe slapped him on the back. "You're all right, for a Frenchie." He looked down the avenue and said, "How's about I take this side of Esplanade?"

"I'll take the other side."

They met three blocks later outside another saloon. Neither had come up with anything useful. Dugas had made a cursory stop at Pane Fresco and found Alessio Alcamo behind the counter, the man more in a daze than yesterday.

After Dugas bought him another beer, Donahoe assured him he would continue asking about the blond man. "I'll see if I can top what you done." Donahoe grinned and strolled away, swinging his billy.

Dugas went back up Esplanade, crossed the Bayou St. John bridge to the park and asked four couples about the blond man and showed them Maria's picture before exiting the park through the new Alexander Street gate. He looked up at the black wrought-iron gate as he passed through it, at the curved, white wrought-iron letters above announcing: New Orleans City Park.

Dugas limped across the road to a long, two-story wooden building with a pitched roof at the confluence of three thoroughfares – Metairie Road, Alexander and Dumaine Streets. On the second story balcony, which wrapped around the corner of the building, Dugas spotted several couples dining. He felt his stomach rumble as he looked up at the sign out front: Jean Marie Saux's Coffeehouse.

Stepping inside, Dugas was assailed by wonderful cooking scents and was led to a small table against a window along the Metairie Road side of the restaurant. His ankle hurt even more now. He was brought a cup of strong coffee-and-chicory immediately by a mousey, brown haired waitress who handed him a menu.

Dugas asked. "What's your name?"

"Alice, sir."

"I've heard the sandwiches here are particularly good."

Alice looked away from Dugas's eyes and nodded. He closed the menu and asked, "Which is the best?"

"Fried oyster sandwich. Best in town."

"Good, I'll have one."

It came quickly. He waited until Alice returned to re-fill his water, as he was half finished the sandwich, to ask about blond haired customers.

"I don't understand, sir."

"Is the manager available?"

"The owner is." Alice hurried off.

Jean Marie Saux was a full-figured woman with long

brassy red tresses piled high on her head. Dugas stood as she arrived. She was around forty, trying her best to look younger with plenty of make-up on her face. She was an attractive woman with a soothing voice and wore a snug-fitting dark green dress. When Dugas showed her his badge, she smiled wickedly and pulled out the chair across from the detective.

She allowed him time to come around and hold the chair for her before sitting. The strong perfume she wore momentarily blotted out the food smells. Alice brought her a coffee and refilled Dugas's cup. He waited until both finished mixing cream and sugar in their coffees before bringing out Maria's photo.

"Yes," said Jean Marie. "She comes here. Quiet a lovely."

Dugas went through the logical series of questions and learned Maria had been in often, usually in the afternoons or early evenings and alone most of the time. When pressed as to when Maria wasn't alone, Jean Marie called Alice over to look at the picture.

"Yes, mum. I've seen her but she come alone."

"Did she ever leave with anyone?" Dugas asked, then mentioned the blond haired man for the first time with Jean Marie at the table. Both women shook their heads, Jean Marie adding, "We have many blond haired male customers."

Then she called over the remaining waitresses, one at a time. The last one, a pretty young woman with reddish brown hair and freckles recognized Maria and when asked about the blond haired man, said, "Funny you asked. One of our regulars hasn't been in today or yesterday. A blond man."

"What man?" asked Jean Marie.

"Why Mr. Vitter. Tall man, always dresses nice, wears the frilly shirts."

Dugas had his note pad and pencil in hand and asked the freckle-faced girl her name.

"Kay Alford, sir."

Dugas stood and pulled a chair out for Kay. "Have a seat."

She waited for Jean Marie's nod of approval before sitting. Dugas sat and said, "Tell me about this Mr. Vitter."

"Bill Vitter, sir. He lives over on Encampment Street. A two story house, white with blue trim, the only house with a fenced yard right off Esplanade."

Jean Marie's eyebrows rose. "And how do you know that?"

Kay blushed, shrugged and looked at Dugas. "What else do you want to know, officer?"

Apparently Bill Vitter had begun frequenting Jean Marie Saux's Coffeehouse about a month earlier, came in every day around noon to stay an hour. Maria came in less frequently and always alone. Kay never saw them together but surmised it could have happened easily. "Mr. Vitter. He's a charmer."

IT WAS A LONG SHOT, BUT AS SOON AS VITTER OPENED HIS door, Dugas felt all the painful limping was worthwhile.

Bill Vitter stood six-two, weighed a good two-hundred pounds which looked to be solid muscle. Dressed in a dark blue suit and matching tie with a frilly shirt, Vitter had his black derby in hand, a row of suitcases lined behind him in the foyer.

"Where's the hansom?" asked Vitter, looking past Dugas,

obviously looking for a cab. When he looked back at Dugas, the detective opened the lapel of his coat. Vitter's blue eyes moved to the badge and he took a hesitant step back, his face suddenly pale.

"Going somewhere, Mr. Vitter?" Dugas took a step inside as Vitter backed away, bumping into the suitcases.

"I'm… going to visit a sick aunt."

"Where?"

Vitter looked behind Dugas again, backed around the suitcase and bolted through the foyer. Dugas limped after him, down a hall, through a formal dining room and into the kitchen, pulling out his revolver as Vitter opened the back door and leaped down the back steps into the yard.

Dugas felt his ankle give out as he hurried down the steps. Falling to his knees in the grass, he watched Vitter put a hand up on the wooden fence and easily clear it. By the time Dugas reached the fence Vitter was gone.

Hobbling back to the house, Dugas moved through to the front porch, then gingerly down to the street, pulling out his police whistle and blowing it until he spotted a beat cop come around from Esplanade. He waved the man over and went back into the house.

Donahoe arrived a few minutes after the first copper and both cops went looking for Vitter while Dugas searched the house. At first he couldn't place the smell that permeated the house but thought it was coppery, like the scent of blood, or maybe it was the copper pipes. He found no trace of blood in the sink or bathtub. In the study he discovered check stubs. Vitter worked for a Canal Street Jewelry Store. No wonder he didn't pry Maria's ring from her finger. A jeweler would know it wasn't worth much, thin as it was, and probably easily identified.

Dugas left the suitcases last to be searched and moved to them as Donahoe returned, wiping his brow with the gray handkerchief and announcing Vitter had disappeared.

"We'll put out a bulletin for him," said Dugas as he spotted a small pool of liquid next to thickest suitcase. He opened it and found Maria's head in a burlap sack.

"My God!" Donahoe moaned, then ran outside to throw up over the porch rail.

O'Meara and McCandless arrived just before the coroner's man. Taking charge, as if he knew anything about the case, O'Meara bossed around the curious patrolmen as they arrived, like moths drawn to a lamp, even tried bossing around the coroner's assistant who ignored him. The police photographer arrived and the coroner's man propped up the head for him to photograph. Dugas took down the everyone's names for his report before checking the other suitcase for more body parts. Nothing but men's clothes. The coroner left with the suitcase containing Maria's head.

McCandless hustled off to the Central Police Station to issue the bulletin on Vitter to be distributed to every precinct and to send telegrams to all surrounded jurisdictions. Dugas made one more careful search before locking up Vitter's house with the keys he found in the front door lock. He watched O'Meara holding a conference with the newspapermen assembled outside Vitter's house as he walked over to Esplanade Avenue and Pane Fresco.

"Dugas," Donahoe called out, jogging to catch up. Huffing

as he arrived, hands on knees. "I'd appreciate it…if you wouldn't tell the fellas…about me…throwing up."

"Of course not."

Donahoe put a friendly hand on Dugas's shoulder as he stood up, taking in a deep breath. "Gotta hand it to you. You solved it."

"Hand it to me?"

Donahoe's eyes lit up and he shook his head. "You know what I mean." He patted the detective's shoulder, turned and headed back up the avenue.

Dugas didn't want Alessio to read about it in the papers. Bad enough the poor man would have to go the coroner's office to identify Maria's head.

Wednesday, 17 June 1891

It was McCandless who caught Bill Vitter at the Carrollton Train Station. Vitter, wearing a long coat on a steamy morning, still wore his ruffled shirt and shiny black shoes. He surrendered without resistance.

"Good work." Dugas patted Mac on the back as he led Vitter into the same interview room where he'd interviewed Alcamo.

"What's this all about?" Vitter said as Dugas sat across from him with a tablet of ruled paper and two fountain pens. Vitter was trying the outraged-citizen defense. Dugas began slowly, introducing himself then asking what Vitter had done Sunday, June fourteenth.

Vitter looked at the blank wall and said that was so long ago he didn't remember. The innocent-disinterested defense. Vitter went through several defensive positions even going so far as to say, "Maria who?"

Dugas fought hard not to reach over and strangle the bastard and had to steel himself to being friendly with his monstrous murderer.

"Don't sit there and tell me you don't know anything about this."

Vitter looked at the other wall.

"I find you standing next to a suitcase with a woman's head in it and you say, 'Maria who?'." Dugas stood up, acting impatient now. "If you don't want to tell your side of the story, that's your choice. I know what you did. You want to give a statement so the jury will hear your side of the story, I'm here to take it down. If not, we'll go right over to parish prison."

Dugas leaned on the table with both hands. "You don't have to testify at your trial, you know that. This might be the only time the jury will hear your words."

Vitter finally looked at Dugas and said, "It was an accident."

A confession was worth the heartache, worth the pain in Dugas's chest as he wormed the story from Vitter. Dugas put Maria's ring and portrait on the table as Vitter told his story. The killer wouldn't look at them at first. By the end of his tale, Vitter was holding the ring and staring at the photo, tears in his eyes.

And who said alligators couldn't cry? Or was it crocodile tears?

Bill Vitter had seen Maria Alcamo at Jean Marie Saux's Coffeehouse on several occasions. She was always alone and didn't meet his eye as most other women who were alone did. Eventually she met his eye, Saturday evening, and when she left he followed her across to the park. Beneath the Alexander gate, he greeted her, tipping his hat and asked if he could walk with her through the park. She went willingly to his house and spent the weekend with him. Sunday evening, she turned on him, becoming abusive, demanding money.

"She struck me and I struck her back and she fell and didn't get up." Vitter stared at the portrait as he softly spoke, "It was an accident."

Dugas kept his face expressionless, hoping Vitter couldn't hear the stammer of his heart, see the loathing in his eyes.

"Then what did you do?"

"I had no choice. I had to get rid...I had to get her out of my house."

Dugas copied the words verbatim.

"So what did you do?"

"I took her apart."

Jesus, such a nice phrase for dismembering someone.

"What did you do with the pieces?"

Vitter swallowed and said he put the pieces in a trunk and took the trunk to the lake, using his neighbor's wagon, and threw the trunk into the water.

"What about Maria's head?"

Vitter blinked at him and said nothing.

"Were you keeping it as a souvenir?"

Vitter looked away again and Dugas knew he'd hit home. He went on to ask where Vitter was going when he came to the door. The sick aunt story again. Dugas tried to get details but the man was vague as to his aunt's name, saying she lived in small town in Mississippi. He couldn't recall the name of the town either.

"How would you get there without knowing the name?"

Vitter picked up Maria's ring and stared at it. Dugas wrote 'no response' next to that question on the statement.

"What about the second trunk, the portmanteau with the clothes in it?"

Vitter nodded. "I forgot to throw her clothes away so I put them in an old portmanteau and tried to throw it in Bayou St. John only some men were there, so I just dropped it."

"Why did you put the hand in the portmanteau?"

"Hand?" He could see Vitter was confused.

"Her left hand," Dugas said. "Where do you think I found the ring?"

Vitter sat frozen, staring at Dugas, the man having no idea how Maria's hand had fallen in the portmanteau as he was getting rid of her clothes. Vitter closed his eyes. Dugas kept his open but could see, in his mind's eye, Vitter frantically cleaning up the blood, tossing body parts into the trunk, tossing clothes into the portmanteau, Maria's hand falling in with the clothes that bore her laundry mark.

"It was an accident," Vitter concluded as he signed his statement.

Accident? Wait until the jury sees the photos of Maria's head.

Dugas watched him sign each page, knowing it would hang him. Watching the man's neck snap would be Dugas's only relief from the pain in his chest.

He looked again at Maria's portrait, at the mischievous glint in her dark eyes and felt sick. It wasn't enough to just catch her killer. As he stood up, he was glad he'd left his revolver out in his desk. Maria seemed to look back at him and he felt a heartache. Maria Alcamo was twenty years old.

Thursday, 18 June 1891

McCANDLESS CAME UP TO DUGAS'S DESK WITH A NOTE IN flowing script.

"Just came by post. It's perfumed," he said, handing Dugas the note, moving around so he could read it too. Dugas opened it and both read:

Dear Detective Dugas,

Hope you won't think me as too forward but I haven't been able to stop thinking about your dark brown eyes.

You know where to find me,

Kay Alford

McCandless slapped Dugas's shoulder. "You hound!"

Dugas tried to compose himself as McCandless walked away, calling over his shoulder, "Better watch yourself with a woman named Alford. That's a Scottish name."

MICHAEL WARREN LUCAS

Michael Warren Lucas might have one of the most twisted and innovative minds in fiction that I have had the pleasure to read. He has published over thirty books in all sorts of areas, from science fiction to fantasy to thrillers to non-fiction and just about everywhere between.

Michael has a way of describing things that just makes you go "What?" and yet at the same time you can see exactly what he is talking about. He does that to a level in this story I have not seen before. You will be shaking your head in wonder by the third paragraph and then it goes from there.

For more of his wonderful writing and nonfiction books, go to https://mwl.io/

THE RATS' MAN'S LACKEY AND THE BRINGER OF LEAVES

MICHAEL WARREN LUCAS

Whackadoo Manor was least creepy at sunrise.

The sideways light highlighted the bright white gingerbread scrollwork that framed the broad full-circle porch and surrounded the windows and eaves. The antique glass in the windows rippled into rainbows that shifted with my every step. The place always looked like a talented Victorian carpenter with a fanatical devotion to magic mushrooms had been given a lifetime supply of wormwood-laced absinthe and all the lumber he could scroll-saw, but this morning the sprawling mansion looked like it might actually be large enough to hold half of the rooms within. Even the leaded-glass conservatory loomed along the side opposite the driveway, and that place almost never deigned to show up.

It might have looked homey, if the edge of my vision hadn't kept catching extra colors in the rainbows.

Wilting hostas, drooping azaleas, and drying coneflowers

surrounded the porch, a fading barricade against the rich green clover meadow that stretched out to the distant tree line. Short, solid Cheery had laid out hedge trimmers and paper bags and leather gloves and the gel-fueled flamethrower near the front flowerbed. She was pulling on the bright yellow bomb suit with the sigil-embossed face shield and the dodo bone belt, so I guessed that the dying greenery objected to today's plan.

Georgia gets its fall late, but the acres of trees surrounding our home away from hell had finally transformed into a glorious spray of red and orange that burned against the morning's piercing blue sky. It wasn't quite cool enough for my breath to turn to steam, but crisp enough to take the edge off today's long run.

I smelled of coffee.

My nameless but disgusting boss sprawled on a porch glider, tucked beneath a threadbare blanket cradling a steaming mug in his gaunt hand. If I took too much interest he might prevent my run for the fourth day in a row, so I spent a few breaths leaning into my hamstrings instead. I felt logy from nine hours of dreamless sleep, my legs and back unwilling to flex, but they'd loosen up soon enough once I started moving.

Five miles in my steel-reinforced buskins and thirty-pound pack, a couple hours on the basement mats and heavy bag, and I'd be ready for breakfast.

So long as he didn't call me back with some ridiculous assignment.

It's what I agreed to—sorry, covenanted. I spent years working for nameless agencies, putting down evil people so that regular families could have jobs and kittens. You can't do that work without hard-headed realism and a complete lack of belief in wizards and demons and all that stupidity. That last assignment showed my realism didn't stretch far enough.

Monsters are real.

Whackadoo Manor is like supernatural Witness Protection; agree to his terms, and he will shelter you.

I don't mind the terms. Or the work. I mind the fubar, all the things that aren't possible in any sane world but exist anyway.

Just as I dared to think I might get today's run, he murmured "Company."

My teeth clanged.

The first time I drove up to Whackadoo Manor, in a half-eaten sedan with something I couldn't see or touch but decidedly real chomped hard into my soul, that drive ambled more than ten miles through the woods. But a hundred feet up our drive was this skinny guy. Beneath a spray of tangled gray hair, his face looked ready to chew ass and spit bacon. Running shoes although his sweats were too clean. Maybe his run had been cut off, too.

I forced out a breath.

The way the visitor was storming up, he couldn't have marched far without getting sweaty.

I dropped my pack and met the guy halfway, calling, "Hello."

The man spat, "Where the hell am I?"

"You're at our home."

"There's no place like this anywhere near here," the man said.

I shrugged. "You've found us. How can we help you?"

He bared his teeth. "Point me back to Pauline."

"Who's Pauline?"

"Pauline Boulevard."

I blinked. "Where are you looking for?"

He snapped, "Stadium Boulevard, then."

I shook my head slow. "Who are you trying to find?"

"I'm trying to get home," the man snapped.

This didn't match any other client we'd had. "I think you better see the boss."

"I don't want to talk to your boss." The man tugged a slim phone out of his pocket. "My phone's busted. It says I'm in Georgia."

We're an hour away from Atlanta—and we most definitely are not. "That's because you're in Georgia."

"Bullshit." His glare had talent, but no training. "I went for a hike around Eberwhite Woods. I'm not even a mile from home."

"Where is Eberwhite?"

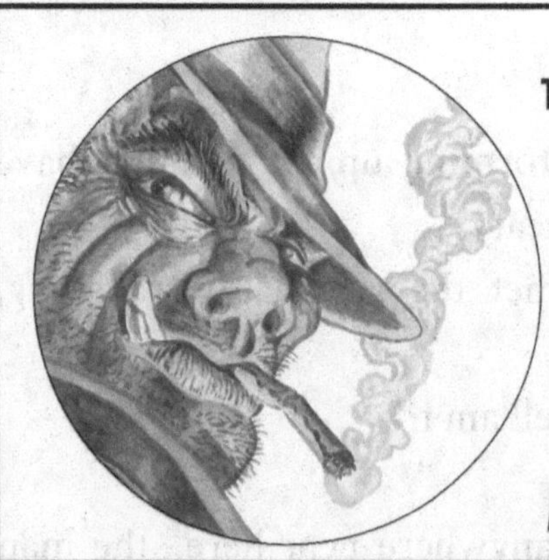

"On Pauline, off Stadium." His eyes narrowed at my blankness. "West Ann Arbor."

I itched to know how someone could stray in here but if I asked the boss, he might tell me. "Look. You can come talk to us and we'll figure this out, or the driveway's right there."

The man glared left and right, as if he might will Ann Arbor to appear. "Fine. Let's talk."

"What's your name?" I said.

"Wallis. Wallis Spatchcock." His face twisted. "I'm sorry for being rude."

"Eh." You can't tell a man you knew he was scared. "You're lost and frustrated."

"What's your name?"

Here we went. "People call me Luggage."

Before I could say our names are picked at random from a list of Terry Pratchett characters Wallis snorted and said, "So you know all about getting lost."

One day I have got to read one of those books. "Sure."

By the time we got to the porch, he had set his coffee to on the side table and tugged the blanket down to his waist. His paper-white skin was stretched tight over starvation-sharp cheekbones, although he eats more than any three people. A smear of last night's beef gravy had dried on his cheek. His pale hair stood every which way, drifting despite the still air. The 1990 Beatles Reunion Tour T-shirt looked like it had toured the inside of an alligator, but at least it didn't have holes. Also fortunately, the blanket in his lap concealed whatever ragged ruin he was passing off for pants.

"This is Wallis Spatchcock," I said. "He went for a walk and got lost."

"Hello," Willis said.

"Mister Spatchcock," he said. "Your grief is an anchor on your heart."

My hollow gut flared. Spatchcock might not have looked for us, but I was suddenly certain he needed us.

Spatchcock's face flared red. Through a tight mouth he said, "I know you want to help. Everybody knows. But I can't stomach any more sympathy. I just want to go home. Can I borrow your phone to call a taxi?"

That's one of Whackadoo Manor's rules. "We don't have a phone," I said.

"Everybody has a phone," he snarled.

"Do you have any signal?" I said. "Or see any wires?"

Spatchcock glared at my waist like he expected to see a lie. A glance at Cheery in her hazmat suit made him stop. "Is— what are those?"

"What are what?"

"Those can't be hostas. They're not even plants."

The way the greenery clawed at Cheery's gloves didn't worry me, but I'd never before let myself notice the tiny keening noises they made as she lopped off the dying leaves.

"Mister Spatchcock," he said.

Spatchcock jerked his gaze back. Fresh sweat trickled down his forehead, and hints of worry had begun to crack his snarl. "Look. I just need to get home. I left the oven on. Can you help me?"

The blanket on his lap stirred. A tiny whiskered nose poked into the light.

"It's all right, Mister Braithwaite," he said, reaching a

famine-ravished finger to stroke the furry muzzle. "Mister Spatchcock won't hurt you."

Spatchcock froze. "Is that a gerbil?"

I said, "Pet rat." One of fifty, maybe a hundred in his office. They have a valet.

Spatchcock drew a shuddering breath. "Home. I need to get home."

He said, "You walked out of your house this morning and discovered a problem."

Spatchcock swelled again. "How do you know that? Did you do it?"

"I did not," he said. "But we can not only take you safely home, we can discover who undid your hard work."

Spatchcock said, "If you know, tell me!"

He uncovered a little more of the rat, stroking down the furry spine. The rat spread himself into a luxuriating pool of shimmering fur. "I fear it is not that simple."

It never is that simple. Not here.

"Yes it is," Spatchcock said.

His voice took on a sing-song tone that always set my teeth on edge. "I will agree to return you home, identify the entity who undid your labors of yesterday, and ensure that they cease their disruptions. In return, you will give Luggage here one well-baked stolen apple crisp."

Spatchcock's eyes bugged. "Go fuck yourself!"

"This agreement is inseverable, all or nothing," he said, but Spatchcock was already whirling away.

My feet shifted, but what was I going to do? I don't kidnap people—the woman who'd stolen the weaponized cholera doesn't count.

He said, "Let him go."

My hands itched. Spatchcock knew he had trouble, but not how fubar it was. Letting him walk away unprotected violated every instinct.

Spatchcock had gone fifty feet when he murmured, "Go on your run."

"We can't just—" I said.

"The man cannot listen now," he said. "Go on your run. Work your heavy bag, your two hundred falls. Bathe and breakfast. A few hours on foot, and he will accept."

For some visitors, Whackadoo Manor's driveway was a few hundred feet. Spatchcock was getting an extra long route.

I shook my head. "As long as I've been here, you have never forced anyone to accept one of your covenants." Not even me. "I won't let you trap that man."

His thin smile exposed ragged yellow teeth. "Not even for the paltry price of a fresh-baked stolen apple crisp?"

"I don't care if it's an apple seed," I said.

"My dear Luggage," he said. "Do you know why I put up with you?"

"Don't change the subject."

The smile evaporated. "Spatchcock will not covenant with me. It will be a mere verbal agreement. With you."

I blinked. "How is that supposed to work?"

"If it doesn't," he said, "he will return for a covenant with me. After sufficient suffering. Dress casual."

———

A FIERCE WORKOUT AND FIERCER SHOWER, A THOUSAND calories of professionally-prepared western omelet and home fries and sliced fruit, and visits to You Bastard the quartermaster and Nobby the mechanic left me with a few trinkets in my pockets and an unremarkable large-but-not-elephantine Subaru SUV. Nobby had done a good job putting the engine back in the chassis after last week's job, and he'd perfectly mended the fang punctures in the passenger door. I held the SUV to a five-MPH idle, drifting down the drive into the woods.

The woodland surrounding Whackadoo Manor is magnificent. Gently rolling hills, old-growth forest so thick you can't get through it without a machete, fearless squirrels and the occasional deer or groundhog. I'd seen a bison, a gazelle, a couple camels. A lynx wandered in once, and I'd had to trank it and haul it into Atlanta so Animal Control could do something with it. I'd been tempted to let it roam, but it would probably have eaten the colony of rockhopper penguins that nest by the meremadillo pond.

I shouldn't have been so surprised that Spatchcock walked in here.

Once the curve of the road put a belt of thick woods between me and the house, I wasn't surprised to see Spatchcock walking down the middle of the road. Four hours, and he hadn't gotten a quarter of a mile. He'd walked further, I was sure. He just hadn't gone further. Whackadoo Manor is pure fubar.

The verge was tall brown grass and wildflowers. I pulled the car to the side, rolled up alongside him, and lowered the window. The Subaru idled faster than he walked, so I rode the brake to keep pace.

Fatigue scored Spatchcock's face, but the embers of his anger still chained his tongue.

"It's gonna take you a long time to walk down this road," I said.

Silence.

"I have sandwiches," I said. "Made by a real chef."

He kept his face forward.

"A jug of water," I said.

Spatchcock's eyes flicked at me, then back.

"Coffee."

Spatchcock stopped so quick, I couldn't stomp on the brake fast enough. "There is no way there's a sixteen mile driveway anywhere around here!"

"Sixteen miles?" I said. "Your GPS works?"

"I average four miles an hour," Spatchcock said.

"And it's been four hours." I took a deep breath. "I hate to say it, but you're not even a quarter mile down this road."

He rolled his eyes.

"Don't believe me?" I put the car in park and turned off the engine. "Let's take a walk back. Just past that bend in the road. If I'm wrong, I will give you a ride home and not say a word. If I'm right, you tell me what your problem is and I see how I can help."

Spatchcock's mouth twisted like he tasted sewage.

"Either way you get a ride home," I said.

"Fine," Spatchcock spat.

Hopping out of the car I said, "Just to that bend. You see where it starts to curve back? By that bright red oak should do it."

I had to stretch my legs to keep up.

But when Spatchcock hit the curve and glimpsed Whack-adoo Manor around the trees, his expression shattered. "That's—not possible."

"I hate fubar," I said.

"Fubar?"

"Fouled Up Beyond All Recognition," I said. "Fubar. Things that don't make sense."

He shook his head.

"If you're fubar," I said. "If you're desperate enough. If it is absolutely the worst day of your life, you can find Whackadoo Manor. You can bargain for help. And, if there's any hope at all, he sends me out to retrieve your life."

Spatchcock shook his head. "The worst day of my life was a month ago. I don't have anything like that."

"Do you want that ride?" I said.

He shook his head, but in denial rather than refusal. "I need something to drink."

"Water?"

"Coffee."

Water would have been smarter, but the chef's coffee is excellent.

I let Spatchcock settle into the passenger seat, pour a cup of coffee out of the insulated flask, and take a sip before saying, "Okay. My boss knows things. I—do not. What's the problem?"

Spatchcock snorted and took another sip. "My wife has been dead for forty-three days. My sweet Jenna. The reason I bother living. Gone. What do you think you can do?"

At least you found someone. I shoved the thought back under its rock and gentled my voice. "That sucks. I'm sorry. That's not what I mean, though. You showed up mad. Something set you off today."

Spatchcock lifted the coffee and grimaced. His dehydrated body had caught on that liquid was available, and he couldn't chug coffee. I raised the jug of water. "Help yourself." He sucked a good pint out without stopping for breath, releasing it with a gasp. "That's better." I let him catch another breath and said, "What happened?"

His lips tightened. "Someone put my leaves back." My expression must have shown my confusion. "I spent all day yesterday raking leaves. My Jenna always likes our yard tidy before the snow comes. I put everything in bags so the city would pick them up."

Normal things for normal people. I nodded.

"Last night," Spatchcock spat, "someone emptied all those bags and put the leaves back. Left the empty bags at the curb."

I frowned. Silly vandalism shouldn't bring someone to us.

"I'm sure it was my neighbor," Spatchcock said. "He's always going on about how we need leaves to stay on the ground so bugs have a place to winter, and I get it, but Jenna wants it tidy so that's it." He downed a gulp of cooling coffee and his stomach grumbled, loud.

I handed him a sandwich wrapped in wax paper. "Our chef made this for you."

Spatchcock narrowed his eyes, but took it. "You knew— this fubar, you knew I couldn't walk out of here."

"He knew," I said. "When I saw you, I figured it out."

"Fine," he said, unwrapping the sandwich. The aromas of fine mustard, fresh home-baked bread, and excellent sharp cheese drifted out. "Take me home. You can go yell at my neighbor and get out. Will that make you happy?" He chomped on the sandwich like it had killed his wife, but immediately slowed. "That's good."

"Our chef is excellent." I started the car. "When I get you home, I'll sort out your leaves."

Spatchcock nodded and engulfed another bite.

I let the SUV idle forward, and the forest changed. Halos of brilliant leaves vanished, leaving bare branches with only tattered brown remnants that would soon break free. The dirt drive became straight asphalt sloping upward, houses on both sides.

Spatchcock coughed, almost spitting his sandwich onto the dash.

"Don't choke," I said.

He forced a swallow. "That's—you can't—it's…."

"Fubar," I said.

Spatchcock worked his mouth. "Fubar."

Cooler air poured through my window. I hurriedly raised the glass—I grew up in the north, but Georgia has spoiled me. "Where's your home?"

"Around the corner." He raised a finger. "That up there, that's Eberwhite Woods. The path in there's a circle. There's no way to get lost. But I wound up at your place."

"Don't think about it too much," I said. "It won't help."

"But—" His phone beeped and buzzed.

"Eat your sandwich," I said. "And tell me which house is yours."

He directed me to one of those two-story 1980s boxes with a uselessly narrow front porch. Those stately decorative pillars that rose all the way to the roof would splinter into kindling at one touch of the Subaru's bumper. The front lawn wasn't large, but with the forest right across the rarely used road you wouldn't need much yard.

I parked in the driveway.

"Thanks for the lift," Spatchcock said, reaching for the handle. "Mind if I take the sandwich?"

"It's yours," I said, "but we have an agreement. I'm investigating your leaves."

"I'm feeling better," he said. "I'm not going to waste your time on a silly prank."

I turned the car off. "If it was silly, you couldn't have found us."

Spatchcock made a face, but rewrapped his sandwich and hopped out.

As he'd said, leaves faded to brown covered the lawn. The air felt humid for autumn, the sun a gray orb that waxed and waned as clouds pregnant with rain scuttled past. The forest's freshness ached in my sinuses, cut with the stink of exhaust and summer's greenery decaying into winter. I grew up in the north, and even after all my time at the manor, this weather made my bones ache for a long-lost home. Before I'd signed up, I had raked yards just like this to earn a few bucks.

The house on our left had a green lawn, with only a few leaves scattered from the forest. The carpet of leaves stretched across the other neighbor's lawn, though.

Spatchcock pointed. "That guy. Right there. Logan. I'm sure it was him."

I nodded. "Why don't you get out of your sweats. You said you'd left your oven on, go take care of that. I'll go talk to Logan."

Spatchcock opened his mouth to argue, but my glare shut him up.

Logan's house was half the size of Spatchcock's and made me think of a brick catbox: taller than it was wide, with a giant front door but meant for one. I rang the bell, triggering a muffled ding-dong somewhere within.

No answer.

I knocked. Rang again. Again. A few minutes of poking the button non-stop, and even the most dedicated hermit would have opened the door just so he could shoot me. Or the fubar had him, and he couldn't answer without bursting into avocados.

The man wasn't home.

I turned to study the yard. My back remembered acres of lawn just like this, covered in dead leaves blown by the wind until they got stuck on other leaves or grass or anything, giving the damp a chance to set in and the leaf mold its opportunity. My palms remembered the burn of the rake handle and blisters that tore before they could fill. Mister Shostakovich at the orphanage had loaned me the rake and told me to wear gloves. If I went back in time to give that young idiot advice, I'd tell him to wear gloves. I hadn't listened to Shostakovich, and I sure wouldn't listen to me.

The lawn itched my memory.

When you shovel leaves into a pile, they get all wet and

stick together. If the bag tears as you're dragging it to the curb, they spill out in grungy clumps. The leaves over Spatchcock's yard were even, the only lumps the natural randomness of fallen leaves. No prankster could have dumped leaves that smoothly.

The yard past Logan's wasn't pristine, but had been raked at least once this season. If someone was going to go environmental vigilante, wouldn't they go after more than one yard?

I walked across the grass, kicking up leaves as I went. No signs of clumps. No change between Logan's yard and Spatchcock's. Fubar itched up my spine. Was there such a thing as leaf fairies? My boss knew. Sometimes he even told, but not in any way that helped until it was almost too late. I better put leaf fairies on my suspect list.

Spatchcock had locked his front door, but a muttered word and two seconds with a Fluffy's-too-old-and-her-meds-are-too-expensive Paw of Glory clicked the tumblers and I sauntered in.

Spatchcock's front room blended tidiness with chaos. The carpet was freshly vacuumed, but a light quilt lay wadded on the couch next to an end table with a crumb-laden plate and empty glass. The ceiling and fireplace mantel had been dusted, but a pair of running shoes lay askew by the door. The vacuum had been steered around the shoes, echoing my teenage years of malicious compliance. The smoke detector had been pulled off the ceiling and the battery removed. A thick scorched stink carbonized the air. Whatever he'd had in the oven had gone to charcoal.

Spatchcock stomped through the arch into the kitchen, wiping his hands on a towel. "I locked that door."

I shrugged. "It opened right up." I should show concern. Try to connect. "Did you take care of the oven?"

"The oven is fine." His voice carried that belligerence. "Did you talk to him?"

"He's not home." The plate didn't just have crumbs. A smear of mayo or mustard or something had become a petrified yellow streak.

"Fine," he said. "You can go."

"I don't break agreements." I let my gaze drift, taking in the heavy curtains pulled tight over the front windows and the modest television. "You say you hadn't gone far, so I must investigate."

"Forget it." Spatchcock tried to keep his voice light, but tension burned beneath. He'd told me the truth, but not enough of it.

"You can't make me break my word." I dug in a pocket and drew out a blue bead on a leather cord. "Hey, do you know what this is?"

Annoyance twisted his face, but he stepped closer. "It's one of those eye things."

An evil eye blurs me from weirdness. Whatever was going on, Spatchcock wasn't trying to curse me. Not with fubar, at least.

"This is my home," Spatchcock said. "Do you want me to call the police?"

"You can." I sauntered to the fireplace. "My ID will make them say yes sir, no sir, as you wish sir." An old photo in a frame of woven silver showed a much younger Spatchcock with a bad case of 90s hair, arm in arm with a beautiful brunette in a voluminous wedding dress. "That's you and

Jenna?"

"It is." Rage rose through his voice. "Get out."

I fixed his gaze with mine. "Tell me what happened to her."

Spatchcock snarled, "Not your business."

"The quickest way to get rid of me is to tell me how she died." Fubar doesn't always involve death. Not always.

Anger made him tremble. "She was baking apple crisp."

What had he said? "Stolen apple crisp."

"That neighbor never picks his apples. They just fall and rot. We go over there after dark, right before that happens, and pick a few. Not all."

Add angry apple fairies to the list. "The neighbor doesn't mind?"

"He never knows. He remembers Kennedy better than our names."

And there's ancient wizard. Weren't there legends about apples? "So she was baking. What happened?"

Spatchcock closed his eyes. "She said it'd be ready in a little bit." His voice sounded like it came from the far side of the moon. "She smiled at me. Then she just fell down. I ran to her." I strained to hear as his words faded. "They said it was a brain aneurysm. Birth defect. It could have failed any time."

"I'm sorry," I said.

"I caught her." Spatchcock was taut as a suspension bridge. "I rolled her onto her back. She breathed out everything. I could smell her last breath. Breathed her into me, and now she's gone." Tears trailed down his cheeks.

The unprofessional but human part of me ached to haul Spatchcock to the nearest bar and pour booze down his throat until that swollen cyst of grief erupted and emptied, but work comes first. Jenna had died in the kitchen, so I'd start there. I slipped past Spatchcock, deeper into the house.

The snug kitchen featured laminate countertops over pressed-wood cabinets that should have imploded decades ago. New electric appliances, a row of ladles and spatulas hanging from overhead cabinets, and cracked beige tile with a pattern that had lost favor before Nixon. The dead interfering with the living never benefits the living, but there weren't any occult symbols or markings of stupid rituals that could hold a spirit to the world. The burned stench scoured my throat.

"Hey!" Spatchcock stomped up behind me, holding a damp red leaf by its stem. "Maybe I can't get rid of you, but I won't have you tracking outside into her kitchen!" Without taking his gaze off me, he meticulously placed the leaf in the open garbage can.

A leaf must have stuck to my foot. "Sorry about that."

"Take those boots off."

Like I'd go barefoot on a job. "Regrowing toes takes too long and itches like hell."

His confusion bought me a breath in the boringly normal kitchen. A cutting board lightly spattered with flour, with a decaying brown heap at one end. He'd vacuumed and scrubbed the counter, but left that goo there? The stove's digital readout read 350, and the BAKE light shone. "Hey." I reached for the button. "The stove's still—"

Spatchcock's face lit in rage as he snatched a rolling pin. "Don't TOUCH THAT!" He swung.

In the service, we'd called that a Number One Strike: a giant looping punch right out of a John Wayne movie. We'd practiced with dull but electrified knives until our bodies responded automatically. My feet shifted, my arms tangled with his, we spun to the ground, then I was sitting on his back with his arm trapped between my thighs and his wrist cranked up by his neck. Satisfaction surged—Whackadoo Manor has many amenities, some of them even sane, but no sparring partners. I always worried that my skills would grow too rusty, but I'd even set him down gently.

Face squeezed against the tile, Spatchcock wheezed.

Fine. Mostly gently.

I peeled the rolling pin out of his limp fingers. Set it aside.

And certainty emerged in a horrifying flash.

"You're okay," I said. "I know where your leaves came from. I won't turn the stove off. I can't turn that stove off." I could, but it would solve nothing. Spatchcock wheezed against my weight. "I'm going to get up now. No more fighting, okay? I don't want to hurt you."

The kitchen floor was tight, but I untangled us without crushing the air out of him too badly. I retreated into the doorway, giving him space to stand. He managed it, eventually.

"You've vacuumed," I said.

Face tight with fear, Spatchcock nodded.

"But you left the shoes by the door."

His jaw clenched.

"That plate in the living room," I said gently. "It was hers. Those shoes were hers. That cutting board. Apple cores. You've left everything exactly as Jenna left it, for forty-three days."

Unshed tears shimmered against Spatchcock's violated rage.

My boss had known. Your grief is an anchor. Not that the bastard would actually tell me.

"And that stolen apple crisp." My heart shuddered. "As long as that oven stays on, as long as that keeps baking, she's still with you."

That's the problem with fubar. You can innocently drop yourself into it. A nervous twitch. A stray joke. Refusing to release even the smallest part of your love can destroy you and your love alike.

I said as gently as I knew how, "Jenna put the leaves back. She's—" screaming? Shrieking? Howling? "—begging you to let her go."

His eyes met mine, but his chin edged back and forth in refusal.

Somewhere distant, a car horn tooted. Then silence.

Spatchcock didn't need me. He needed a headshrinker and meds and his own family. What was I supposed to do, drag him to the psych ward? No, his heart was the anchor.

Between us, the trash rustled.

Trembling, a red leaf edged up out of the can, teetered on the edge, and fluttered to the tile.

Spatchcock stared, jaw hanging open.

My softest tones sound like an order, but I tried. "You've chained her here. She's trapped."

A breeze I didn't feel caught the leaf and brushed it to Spatchcock's toes.

"She could have done anything." I had no idea if she could have done anything else. "But you knew the yard was important to her, so she put it back. She's telling you to move on."

Spatchcock's gaze stayed fixed on the leaf.

It trembled one last time and lay still.

Spatchcock's face twisted like I'd clamped jumper cables to him. He gulped air but wasn't breathing.

I said, soft as I could, "If she could see you now—no. She can see you now."

Spatchcock hugged his chest like he was trying to contain an explosion.

I didn't dare speak another word.

Rocking on his feet, Spatchcock's lips formed soundless words.

He whirled. His hand twitched like broken clockwork. An inch forward, freeze, half an inch back and lurch forward again. An agonizing moment later he a laid finger against the stove's OFF button.

I felt a directionless snap. I still don't know if I'm learning to sense fubar or if it's all in my mind. But he had said the price for my aid was a fresh-baked stolen apple crisp, so I needed the crisp—or, more likely, Spatchcock needed to be rid of it. "Let her go, once and for all. Give me the crisp."

Spatchcock managed to extract the baking dish from the oven before collapsing. The glass had scorched to brown, full of crumbly coal shards that redefined "burnt."

I could do nothing more for Spatchcock. He needed to lie on that floor and sob it out until the grief emptied out and he could start to heal. I borrowed two ragged potholders and carried the dish out of the house and across the tidily raked lawn. The heat radiating off the blackness seemed more penetrating than it should. A surge of wind carried a handful of black dust away, but the petrified remnants went into the back of the SUV.

Flinging the dish in a convenient trash can felt wrong. I took it back to the Whackadoo Manor grounds and buried it, a tiny grave amidst the fading forest, everything dying so it could be reborn. Digging the hole gave me time to think.

He had asked if I knew why he put up with me. Maybe it had been an offhand comment. Maybe, like the anchor comment, it had been a hint. I placed the dish neatly in the hole, waited a respectful breath, and started filling it back in.

We annoyed each other.

We needed each other.

One of us would die first. The other, would mourn.

But not too much.

START HERE

DivingintotheWreck.com

ANNIE REED

Professional writer Annie Reed writes stories that span genres and are always powerful. In fact with Annie, you just never know the type of story you might be reading, but you will always know it will grab you and be a compelling read.

So far Annie has had a story in every issue of this magazine and as the editor, I hope to continue that streak.

Annie's stories have appeared in four best mystery stories of the year volumes so far. Look for so much more of Annie's work at her website https://anniereed.wordpress.com/

THE WALL

ANNIE REED

The morning had turned out unseasonably warm for November, even for Northern Nevada, with not even a hint of a breeze from the foothills to the west. Veteran's Day should be cloudy and cold with the possibility of rain, but the day had dawned sunny. A perfect day for Stan to spend time outside with his grandson in this quiet park just a few miles from the high rises at the center of the city, just like he had when the boy had been little.

Or it would have been if sweat wasn't already trickling down the back of Stan's neck. The small of his back beneath his golf shirt and windbreaker was damp with it. His hands were shaking and his chest felt tight like he couldn't breathe, and he wasn't anywhere near the memorial yet.

He hadn't planned on this visit to the memorial. He wasn't sure he even wanted to be here, not if being here was going to upset him this much. He didn't need to touch the smooth black granite and trace Timothy's name with his fingers to remember the man who'd meant more to him than life itself.

He'd only come because his daughter had asked if he wanted to take Jonathan to visit the Vietnam Veterans' Memorial while it was on display in the park. In her round-about way, what she was really asking him was to get the kid alone and see if he'd open up about where he'd gotten the bruises and cuts on his face and the scrapes on his knuckles.

Not that Jonathan wanted to be here either since he was currently dragging his feet getting out of Stan's car.

Stan could relate. He could always take the boy to break-fast instead, but it felt disrespectful somehow not to at least go look at the memorial now that he was here.

He sighed and tried to get a handle on his emotions. He wasn't normally such a foolish old man. Timothy would have teased him, would have reminded him that the memorial was just a hunk of stone, nothing to get upset about. Vietnam and the war and the ambush where Timothy had died were more than fifty years in the past.

Stan stretched his shoulders and tried to distract himself with mundane things, like whether he should leave his windbreaker in the car. He'd put it on that morning more out of habit than anything else. Golf shirt, windbreaker, and khaki pants with a thin leather belt. Old man clothes. That was his uniform these days. Far removed from the uniform he'd worn for his country.

A car door slammed behind him, and he heard Jonathan scuff his way across the parking lot.

At sixteen, Stan's only grandson was already half a head taller than Stan and skinny as a rail. Not that Stan was all that tall. In his prime he'd never been more than average height, but age and gravity had stolen precious inches along with the flexibility of his spine. These days he felt small, especially standing next to Jonathan.

"Is that why we're here?" Jonathan asked as he stopped next to Stan on the concrete sidewalk encircling the park.

His head was tilted to one side, something Stan thought the boy did to keep his lanky hair off his face. Jonathan squinted and then held one hand up as if to shield his eyes from the sun as he looked toward the center of a large swath of lawn where the memorial had been installed.

The sun was at the boy's back, only a couple of hours above the eastern horizon. The unnecessary gesture was another teenage protest at having to get up and actually do something with his grandfather this early on a school holiday.

The memorial they'd come to see was a half-size replica of the Vietnam Veterans Memorial in Washington, D.C. The replica was made up of black granite panels erected side by side to form two long black wings. Just like the memorial in

D.C., the highest point of the replica was the center. From there, the two wings stretched out at an angle from each other, each wing decreasing in height until the far ends looked like they dug into the wide expanse of lawn where the replica had been erected.

And just like the memorial in D.C., the replica's black granite panels were covered with tens of thousands of names of the dead.

Stan had never been to the original wall. The Moving Wall, as this replica was called, had been created to travel from place to place so that people who couldn't go to the original memorial still had a way to honor soldiers killed in Vietnam.

The memorial looked like a slash of nothingness against all that winter-brown November grass, but it was far from nothing. No matter how much Timothy might have teased him, Stan couldn't deny the power of all the accumulated grief and loss etched into those black granite panels. It stole Stan's breath even half a football field away.

"That's it," he finally made himself say, his voice gruffer than he'd intended.

If Jonathan noticed, he didn't mention it. Most of the time he affected a don't-give-a-shit attitude, but Stan knew better. Teenage boys gave a shit about everything.

The bruise on his grandson's left cheek just below his eye had turned a mottled greenish yellow with a few spots of dark purple where rough knuckles had dug into the kid's face. The scrape on his chin and the cut across the bridge of his nose were healing nicely—he might not even have a scar. At least not one people would be able to see.

"So, what do we do?" Jonathan asked. "Just go look at it?"

If Stan could bring himself to get that close to it. He hadn't expected the memorial to affect him this way.

"That's the general idea," he said, and somehow he got his feet to start moving.

Just like he had all those decades ago.

Keep marching. Keep walking. Keep slogging through the jungle, one foot after the next, and never let yourself wonder if the next step would be your last.

THE GUY AT THE HEAD OF THE PATROL, A TALL BLACK KID FROM Michigan by the name of Jamal Watkins, took the first bullet.

The NVA ambushed them from the trees, shadows in black pajamas hiding in the deeper shadows of the jungle. One minute Jamal was grinning at something the new kid in the company had done, some misstep the kid had made because he was the FNG and didn't know any better, and the next minute blood was gushing from a round that blew through Jamal's right shoulder, taking muscle and bone with it as the jungle around the patrol erupted with the rapid fire of automatic weapons.

Timothy yanked Stan to the ground as mortar shells fell around them sending great gouts of dirt and splintered trees and shattered bodies into the air. A fallen tree gave them the barest amount of cover, but it wasn't enough. A ricochet hit Stan in the upper arm, and his entire arm went numb.

Soldiers shouted instructions to each other and screamed as they were hit. The jungle filled with smoke and gunfire and explosions, and the smell of blood and shit and piss filled the air. NVA dropped from the trees, dead and dying and merely wounded, but they just kept coming and coming.

The enemy knew the jungle, knew how to use it to their advantage. Jamal had been born in fucking Detroit, Stan in Queens. What the hell did they know about jungle warfare? Timothy had been born in Montana, but the jungles of Vietnam were nothing like the pine forests of his home.

The patrol's medic had been among the first to die. Rounds ripped a jagged line through his chest, and he was dead before he hit the ground.

The FNG picked up the medic's kit and tried to help Jamal, but Jamal bled out before the evac helicopter got to them.

Jamal with his wide smile and good heart wasn't the first of their company to die, and he wasn't the last.

Timothy had been the last.

And Stan had been holding Timothy's hand, their fingers intertwined, when the light went out of his eyes.

THE PARK HAD BEEN A WORKING RANCH BACK IN THE DAYS WHEN the handful of buildings clustered near the river could hardly be called a town. As the city grew and the demand for land became intense, the rancher's descendants deeded the ranch to the city on the condition that the city keep the land intact and turn it into a regional park, including a museum honoring their family's contribution to the area.

The city had kept up its end of the deal. The acres and

acres of old pasture land had been planted with grass and trees and landscaped with jogging paths and flower gardens and a meditation area with Japanese maples and dogwoods and a koi pond. The ranch house had been renovated and turned into a museum dedicated to the history and accomplishments of the land's original owners. The north side of the ranch house had been expanded into a high-ceilinged exhibition space for special events.

When Jonathan had been a toddler, Stan had taken him to a dinosaur exhibit in the ranch house. Jonathan had been fascinated with the full-size animatronic T-Rex. Stan had tried to read all the informational placards in the exhibit to the boy, but like any headstrong two-year-old, Jonathan had just wanted to be picked up so he could get closer to the dinosaurs.

That visit had been the only time Stan had ventured into the museum side of the old ranch house. The first two rooms were stuffed to the gills with memorabilia from the ranch—old tack and restored furniture and guns, lots and lots of guns—dating back to the late nineteenth century. A short movie honoring the family's part in establishing the city played on a continuous loop in another small room.

Jonathan hadn't wanted to stay and watch the movie. He'd wanted to see the animals.

Dozens upon dozens of big game trophies from Africa and the Arctic and North America filled the rest of the museum. Apparently the rancher had been a big game hunter in his later years.

All the dead animals with their glass eyes only made Stan sad, especially a mountain lion mounted to a tree limb that appeared to be growing out of a wall. The lion had been posed in mid-snarl, its expression fierce and menacing.

Being fierce hadn't been enough to save the lion's life. There was always someone bigger. Someone with a better weapon. Someone who didn't play by the rules or give a shit about anyone's life but their own.

Vietnam had taught him that. The war and the fallout from the war he'd lived through after he'd returned to the states had left him believing the only way to survive in the world was to blend in, so that's what he'd done for fifty years. Lived his life the way everyone expected him to. One wife, one kid, one grandson, and never a mention of Timothy or the war beyond the fact that he'd been wounded overseas.

The memorial had been set up on the lawn to the west of the ranch house. Maples and oaks, their branches winter bare, lined the edge of the lawn where it sloped down to a marshy area that was the remains of an old irrigation ditch, but no trees shaded the memorial.

Dry grass crunched beneath Stan's shoes as they made their way across the lawn to the wall. The closer they got to the memorial, the more he felt like the world was pressing down on him.

It almost felt like he was buried beneath all that black granite, weighed down by each of those thousands and thou-sands of names inscribed on the stone. They'd died while he'd survived. He thought he'd come to terms with his survivor's guilt years ago, but now he wasn't so sure.

More people than Stan had expected to see this early in the morning were clustered near the memorial. They stood on the lawn in front of the wall, some by themselves, some in small groups. The Vietnam war was ancient history to most people like his grandson. Stan had thought the memorial would attract only a few older men and women who, like him, had survived their time in country or who'd lost loved ones to the war. But a surprising number of middle-aged men and women, some with children younger than Jonathan, had come to pay their respects.

A few people were holding sheets of thin paper against the wall and rubbing crayons or bits of graphite over the paper to make an impression of a name etched in the granite. One young woman only slightly older than Jonathan lay sprawled on her stomach so that she could trace a name close to the ground.

Some people were crying, men and women alike, but Stan's eyes were drawn to a dry-faced man not that much younger than himself.

The man held a toddler with one arm, a blond-haired little boy of no more than two. The man had his other hand on the wall, and the toddler leaned forward to touch the wall next to the old man's gnarled hand.

The toddler's expression was as solemn as the old man's. No tears, no fussing. Just touching the wall with the flat of his hand with something approaching reverence.

Stan couldn't remember ever seeing such a mature look on such a young face.

"Holy shit," Jonathan said, his voice barely above a whisper. "Those are all names."

Over fifty thousand names, Stan didn't say.

"I thought…." Jonathan sucked in his lower lip. "From far away, they just look like lines in the rock. I thought that was pretty stupid, you know? Just a bunch of black rock with a bunch of lines. What kind of a memorial is that? Even tombstones are engraved, but this…."

He shook his head and shoved his hands in the pockets of his jeans. He was far more handsome than Stan had ever been. Stan had never understood what Timothy had seen in him.

Jonathan cleared his throat. "Are you here to see someone?"

Stan had never talked about Vietnam with Jonathan. He'd barely talked about it with his wife, much less their daughter or her husband. He'd been surprised when she'd first suggested that he take Jonathan to the memorial, but then he'd realized she had an ulterior motive.

The fight. Jonathan wouldn't tell his parents what had happened. Stan wasn't sure the boy would tell him either. But Stan's daughter had always been a bulldog with a bone once she got an idea in her head, so he'd agreed.

And now Jonathan was asking if Stan was here to see someone.

He couldn't just turn his back on Timothy and walk away,

even if the only part of Timothy that was left was his name on the wall.

Was he here to see someone? "Yes," Stan said.

He was here to see the only man he'd ever loved.

VIETNAM WAS A SHOCK TO THE SYSTEM. LOUD AND HOT AND steamy, locals constantly trying to sell him booze and drugs and sex. Jostling against him, shoving him and screaming obscenities at him when they thought they could get away with it, and little kids always trying to pick his pockets.

For a kid who'd grown up in Queens, it had been too much.

Even for a kid who'd screwed up his courage once and gone to Stonewall after he got his draft notice and realized that he might die without ever once being kissed like it meant something, Vietnam was too much.

Timothy rescued Stan from that chaos.

He introduced Stan to the pleasure of letting a good book take him to a quieter, better place. Before that, books had been something Stan had to read for school, and that shit was over. Timothy taught Stan chess and how thinking three moves ahead could save him on the battlefield.

"It'll keep that skinny ass of yours alive," Timothy said.

He told Stan stories about growing up in Montana with his dad and older brothers, real mountain men, he called them.

"You weren't?" Stan asked, fascinated with the idea of someone like Timothy, with his deep blue eyes and features that were almost but not quite delicate, might be a mountain man.

Timothy laughed. "I read and I play chess. Sometimes I fish, but that's it. What do you think?"

They became inseparable, the best of buddies. Timothy looked out for Stan when they went into the jungle on patrol. He taught Stan all the things boot camp hadn't, like how to spot NVA hiding places in the tall trees and how best to pack his gear for long treks through the jungle.

And somewhere along the way, Stan realized that they weren't just buddies anymore. The first tentative touches were almost inevitable. Quiet stolen moments where no one else could see.

Decades before don't ask, don't tell, they had to be so very careful. Never saying the words, never letting anyone see what they meant to each other.

Stan had never told Timothy he loved him. Not even when Timothy lay dying in a hot, stinking jungle so far away from his Montana home.

It was the biggest regret of Stan's life.

———

TIMOTHY'S NAME WAS ON THE THIRD PANEL FROM THE END ON the right-hand side of the wall, in a row slightly below shoulder height. If this had been the full-size wall, the name would have been far over Stan's head.

He touched Timothy's name with the kind of gentleness that Timothy had used the first time they'd been together. He traced each letter like the mere touch could bring back the man so Stan could finally, at long last, tell Timothy what he'd felt. What he still felt.

He didn't realize that his face was wet until Jonathan spoke up behind him.

"Grandpa? Are you okay?"

Was he okay?

No, he was far, far from okay, but he had to say something.

"I think you would have liked him." Stan glanced at Jonathan. "He would have liked you."

Jonathan had his hands stuffed in the pockets of his jeans. His don't-give-a-shit expression was long gone.

"He saved my life, you know," Stan said, turning his attention back to the wall. "More than once, but that last time...he got me on the ground, got us both behind cover when all hell broke loose. Saved my fucking life."

MORTARS AND AUTOMATIC GUNFIRE AND THE SMELL OF BLOOD and dirt and jungle rot choking the air, Stan's arm on fire as blood soaked his uniform sleeve. Timothy told him to stay down, just stay the fuck down, but he didn't take his own advice. The radioman had taken a hit, his leg half blown off, his guts shredded by shrapnel.

"I have to call it in," Timothy told Stan. "Call in the evac or we're all going to die out here. You understand?"

"Let me go," Stan said. "You stay here. I'll go."

He tried to get up, but Timothy pushed him back to the ground. "You can't call in the coordinates, you don't know how."

Stan saw the truth of it in Timothy's eyes, and they shared the kind of look men shared when they know their tomorrows aren't guaranteed.

"Just don't die," Stan said.

"Never," Timothy said.

But he had.

He reached the radio, still strapped to the dying radioman's back, and called in their coordinates. Called in a strike and an evac while blood ran down his back from wounds he might have survived if not for the last bullet that blew through his thigh.

Stan saw Timothy go down. By the time he crawled to where Timothy lay, the ground beneath Timothy was soaked with bright, arterial blood.

Stan tried to stop the bleeding, but it was too late. Timothy reached out to Stan with one weak hand, and Stan held it, their bloody fingers threaded together, until long past the time Timothy was gone.

STANDING IN FRONT OF THE WALL, STAN TOLD HIS GRANDSON every last detail that he could remember of that firefight. He owed Timothy that much. "That evac saved the rest of us," he said.

Jonathan didn't say anything for the longest time, but something was going on behind his eyes.

Had Stan said too much? He didn't know.

"He wasn't just another soldier, was he?" Jonathan finally asked.

Stan heaved a deep sigh, his heart beating heavily in his chest. He turned back to the wall and touched Timothy's name. He wasn't about to deny what they'd been to each other. Not here. Not now.

"No," he said. "He wasn't."

The dry grass rustled as Jonathan shifted behind him. The quiet murmur of the other visitors to the memorial blended with the sound of traffic passing by the park a half mile away, but Jonathan said nothing.

The silence between them grew uncomfortably long, but Stan didn't want to break it. Jonathan needed to come to terms with something he'd probably never imagined about his grandfather. If he was anything at all like Stan had been when he'd been sixteen, Jonathan probably didn't like to think about his parents, much less his grandfather, ever having sex.

"You loved him," Jonathan finally said. It wasn't a question.

Stan couldn't deny that either. "Yes," he said. "I never told him, but I think he knew." He hoped Timothy had known.

"Is that…was he the only…?"

There'd been kissing at Stonewall, groping in the back room and sweet release at the hands of a stranger twice his age, but that hadn't been love.

"Yes," Stan said.

Timothy's name was so small on this wall. All the names of the dead were, but to Stan, Timothy had always been so much larger than life. It didn't seem right that his name was so small.

Jonathan stepped closer to the wall until he stood next to Stan. He touched the wall, his fingers not quite on Timothy's name. The scabs on his knuckles stood out against his pale skin.

"Did grandma know?" he asked.

Stan started to shrug and made himself stop. "I left that part of my life behind in Vietnam. Walled it up, told myself it was over. If she knew, she never said. She never asked, and I never told her."

His own version of don't ask, don't tell.

Somewhere in the distance, a dog started barking, high angry yipping barks, and more dogs took up the cry. A slight breeze had just started. It lifted the lank hair that had flopped over Jonathan's forehead.

"Why did you bring me?" Jonathan finally asked.

"It was your mother's idea," Stan said. "She was hoping you'd tell me what happened."

Jonathan had come home late from school a few days ago, his cheek already swelling and threatening to turn into a black eye. He'd flat out refused to tell his parents what had started the fight or even who had been involved.

"It was just a stupid fight." A deep frown creased the boy's forehead, and he sighed. "I don't like bullies."

Stan nodded toward the wall. "He didn't either," he said. "He enlisted, can you believe that? We were being drafted left and right back then, and he enlisted."

Jonathan turned his head to look at Stan. There was no disgust in his eyes, no judgment. "Tell me about him," Jonathan said. "Not the soldier stuff. Tell me who he was."

So Stan did.

As the sun rose higher in the clear November sky, Stan told his grandson all that he could remember about the man he'd loved. The words spilled out of him as more and more memories rose to the surface.

He told Jonathan about how Timothy had grown up with his brothers in Montana. How he'd loved to fish. His brothers loved to hunt but putting worms on the hook always made them squeamish, so whenever their dad took the boys fishing, they always made Timothy do it.

About how his brothers played football, but Timothy went out for track. He'd won medals at district matches, and he wore his letterman jacket with as much pride as his brothers had worn theirs.

About how Timothy never kept his preferences a secret from his family, but he'd kept them hidden from the Army, pretending an interest in women that he didn't feel so that he wouldn't be dishonorably discharged.

"Do you think...." Jonathan paused, clearly trying to figure out how to say what he wanted to ask. "If he had survived, do you think you'd have stayed together?"

That wasn't a question Stan had expected. When he'd been in Vietnam, when their love had been new, Stan had dreamed of a life together after the war, a life where they wouldn't have to hide and lie. A life where they could be themselves. Even then, he'd known it was only a dream, but the dream had kept him going, right up until the day Timothy died.

Stan had been so lost after that, it was a wonder he'd survived. The only reason he hadn't walked in front of an NVA bullet was the knowledge that Timothy had given his life so that Stan could live.

"I don't know," he said. "It was a different time back then. Men like Timothy—men like we both were...." He paused, realizing that was the first time he'd actually said something like that out loud. "Times were tough back then."

"It's not all that different."

There was a dark current of anger in Jonathan's voice. Stan wondered if that was what the fight had really been about, but he wasn't going to ask.

Jonathan would talk about the fight when he was ready. And if he never was? The boy was growing into a man, and men kept secrets. Stan's daughter would have to learn to live with that.

More people were in the park now, filling up the space in front of the black granite panels. A middle-aged woman carrying a white rose crossed behind Stan and Jonathan. When Stan glanced at her, she nodded at him.

"Thank you for your service," she said.

Jonathan frowned after her. "How did she know?" he

asked after she stopped before a low panel two away from where they stood.

Stan had no idea. Maybe it was simply because he was the right age range.

While he appreciated that people felt a need to thank soldiers for their service, the men and women who'd died in Vietnam had been so much more than soldiers. Jonathan had asked him about who Timothy had been as a man. Who he might have been if he'd survived. It had been the kindest thing Stan's grandson had ever done for him.

Timothy would always be so much more than a name on a wall. Stan didn't need to stay here any longer. He'd paid his respects to Timothy, and the grief he'd felt when he'd first come to the park had lifted. He could breathe again.

Stan took a step away from the wall. "How about I buy you breakfast?" he asked his grandson.

Jonathan raised an eyebrow. "You're ready to go?"

Yeah, he was. Timothy had lived on in Stan's memory. Now he'd keep living on in Jonathan's.

"I thought I'd tell you a few more stories," Stan said. "Unless you're all listened out."

For the first time that morning, Jonathan smiled. It was the kind of indulgent smile parents give small children, but Stan would take it.

"No, I'm good to go, Grandpa," Jonathan said.

As they walked across the lawn toward the parking lot, a breeze kicked up from the foothills to the west. The breeze brought a chill with it that felt more like November, and for the first time Stan was glad he'd dressed in his old man's uniform, right down to the windbreaker.

Timothy would have made fun of him if he'd seen Stan in this getup. He might have called himself a mountain man, but Timothy liked fine clothes, and he had a wicked sense of humor.

"Remind me to tell you about the time Timothy put together costumes for his brothers for the school play," Stan said.

The football players had appeared on stage in drag—that time-honored tradition of football players dressing as cheerleaders. According to Timothy, his brothers had been the best dressed cheerleaders in the whole world, thanks to a little judicious altering of their costumes.

Jonathan chuckled. "I can just imagine." Then he scrunched up his nose. "Does mom know?" he asked. "I don't want to screw up and say something if she doesn't."

No, she didn't, but did Stan want to keep hiding this part of his life from her?

"Let me talk to her when we get back to your house," he said. "I don't want you to have to keep my secret."

He didn't want anyone to have to keep his secret. Vietnam was half a lifetime ago, and it was long past time to let this secret go.

He owed it to himself.

Most of all, he owed it to the man whose name was engraved on the wall.

PULPHOUSE KITTY SAYS:
SUBSCRIBE
ebook or paperback
pulphousemagazine.com
Pulphouse
FICTION MAGAZINE

KRISTINE KATHRYN RUSCH

Kristine Kathryn Rusch is a New York Times *and* USA Today *bestselling writer and maybe the most award-winning and prolific writer working today. She has won more awards in science fiction and mystery than just about anyone alive and she is the only person to win the Hugo Award for her writing as well as her editing.*

This story ended up here when Kris dropped the manuscript on my desk and asked "Think you might be interested in this one?"

The manuscript had my handwriting on it. "Great!!!" scrawled across the top. So of course I was interested. The story had amazing heart in many different ways. And yes, I really was the best market for it.

So here it is. Enjoy.

You can find out a lot more about Kris's work at her publisher, WMG Publishing Inc www.wmgbooks.com or her website www.kriswrites.com

THE MIX-UP

KRISTINE KATHRYN RUSCH

Briella Wilder felt silly driving back to the Rolling Hills Pet Memorial Park with the small and tasteful gray bag strapped into the passenger seat of her six-year-old Audi. She had a slight headache from repressing tears which—she thought—was a lose-lose situation. If she cried, then she couldn't see the road. And if she didn't, she got the headache.

Of course, she almost always got a headache after crying, hence lose-lose.

And there really wasn't anyone she could talk with about losing Rochester, not someone who would understand. Her more insensitive friends were impatient with her. After all, she had lost cats to old age before, and she had two perfectly lovely Siamese at home, so, really, what was the problem?

The problem was that Rochester had been beside her for the past fifteen years. He had shown up at her new apartment in her new city, when she had been shaky and terrified to live alone.

Until that summer, she never had lived alone nor had she ever moved across country before. She knew back then that she needed a new start. Her parents had divorced and started new families and she had married the wrong man in the middle of that, maybe to prove to them that marriage worked.

Instead, she had learned that marriage was hard, and she and Del did not love each other enough to weather the ups and downs. He liked to say he left first, but that wasn't accurate. They left together, on the same day, walking down the sidewalk away from the townhouse that had felt so very sterile, the way that people walked down an aisle as they exited a church.

Reverse wedding march, she had called it, and Del had snuff-laughed, something she always liked about him.

She liked most things about him—still did—but she had never really loved him. They had remained friends, though, and he had been the first to call her when she had texted that Rochester died.

Rochester. Hard to believe he fit into the tiny cat-shaped urn Rolling Hills had given her.

Or hadn't fit, as the embarrassed owner of Rolling Hills told her that very morning.

Because the cremains in the urn beside her did not belong to Rochester. They belonged to another cat named Rose Chester. The extremely stressed receptionist had misheard, and given Briella the pretty little gray bag without following procedure.

No doublecheck on the last name, no need to present identification. Just Briella's signature on a fancy little document, and then the receptionist had gone into the back and returned with the gray bag, that Briella had somehow known from the beginning did not belong to Rochester.

But she had assumed she had felt that way because Rochester was gone. He had struggled so hard at the end—a bony pile of long black fur which was steadily getting coarser due to illness, pretending that everything was all right, until he couldn't anymore.

Even then, on that last morning, he had gotten up off his special catbed (which Briella had moved to the end of the couch during those final two weeks so that he could always be with her) to greet the home-care vet who was going to put him out of his misery.

He had toppled over on his way to her, and Briella had to pick him up, cradling him as she talked to the vet. It was obvious to all three of them that Rochester had used up all of his nine lives and then some.

Briella's two Siamese—Brooklyn and Bronx—watched from their favorite hiding place under the stairs. They were a bonded pair that had met at the animal shelter and taken to each other. They liked Rochester, but they had never loved him.

Not like she had.

She swiped at her left eye, because it was betraying her by filling with tears. Fortunately, she had turned on the wide side street that led to the memorial park.

The park was startlingly big, partly because it was almost as old as the city. The park was green, with actual rolling hills and large pine trees. There was a manmade pond in the center, with benches all around it. The benches had iron railings that were decorated with little cat and dog heads. The feet were, of course, clawed.

She had gone into the park three days after Rochester died and sat quietly, staring at the pond. That was the day Rolling Hills had called to let her know that his remains were ready. Or cremains, as they insisted on calling them.

She had gathered herself enough to go inside the little white building, when a couple stormed out, still screaming at each other. She had hoped for peace, and had instead found turmoil.

Turmoil everywhere.

And the poor receptionist tried her best that day. She had been shaking from the encounter, trying not to cry herself, and yet somehow remaining professional. She had even—with empathy—told Briella that she was ever so sorry for her loss.

Briella had believed her. But Briella had never believed that the little urn held her heart-cat. And she had told herself that the reason was because she had never received the cremains of a cat before, even though she had cremated three others.

She just couldn't bear to part with whatever was left of Rochester. And yet, it turned out, she had.

She pulled into the narrow parking lot in front of the white building. There was another, wider lot, for people who wanted to visit their pets in the cemetery. She had seen the little headstones, some with lifelike statues of a cat or a dog or, in one case, a rabbit, but she couldn't imagine leaving Rochester there. That felt like abandoning him.

He had hated the outdoors so very much. He never wanted to leave the warmth and safety of indoors, not after she had rescued him.

Another car, a newish dark blue sedan, sat at the other side of the narrow parking lot. For a moment, Briella stared at the vehicle, trying to see if someone was inside. As emotionally fragile as she was at the moment, she didn't really need to see another screaming fight outside of this building.

But the car appeared empty, and it was parked far away enough that it might have belonged to a staff member.

Briella sighed, and stepped out of her car into the spring sunshine. The sun wasn't warm, but its thin light was comforting. She wiped at her eyes again, then reached back inside the car and removed the tasteful gray bag.

The braided handle was soft between her fingers, and the bag itself was thick and pleasant to the touch. It struck her that this was not the type of place that made obvious mistakes, particularly ones that would cause the pet parents even more grief.

The owner had to have been mortified.

Briella took a deep breath, and crossed the lot. Last time she had been here, two days ago, she hadn't noted how clean the white exterior was or the beautiful calligraphy in the same gray as the bag which suggested the rolling hills of the business's name.

She opened the door and stepped inside, then blinked at the sudden dimness. It took a moment for her eyes to adjust.

The entry was clean and wide, with a few seats along one wall. There were pamphlets on grief and a display of urns that looked like they had been taken from a museum.

A small door opened into a hallway Briella had never ventured down. If the tiny map on the corner of the desk was accurate, they included viewing rooms and places for families to mourn, just like a human mortuary had.

A man was standing near the reception desk, blocking Briella's view of the receptionist. The man was wearing a shirt that stretched across his broad shoulders. His dark hair rested on the back of his collar a bit unevenly, suggesting that it needed a trim. He was taller than she was and looked strong, but nothing in his posture suggested that he was angry.

Briella hung back, so that she wouldn't call attention to herself. At first, she thought there was going to be conversation, but there wasn't: no one sat in the reception chair.

A woman that Briella hadn't seen before came out of the

back area, and said as she did, "Mr. Chester, if you'll just wait in the back. It'll take a minute—"

"Mr. Chester?" Briella blurted before she could stop herself. "You're Rose's…"

She let the name dangle, because she wasn't sure what to call him. Some people objected to *owner*. Others thought *pet parent* too precious by half.

The man turned. He had a strong face, with flat cheekbones and a square jaw. His skin was light brown and he had deep circles under his eyes.

He looked as sad as she felt.

"Yes?" he asked.

She held up the bag. "I think this might be yours."

"Let me." The receptionist hurried over and took the bag. She was an older woman, wearing tan dress pants and a blue and tan patterned blouse that would hide any stain.

Briella recognized her voice. This was the woman who had called that morning.

"Let's get you to the back room," she said. "I need to confirm…"

And then she shook her head, as if somehow, she was editing the experience as she was having it.

"I'm so sorry about the confusion," she said. "We don't run our business like this. I don't know what happened, but I can assure you, it won't happen again."

"I know what happened," Briella said. "You had a couple in here that was having a screaming fight over their pet. I got the sense they were no longer together. It felt…"

She wasn't sure how to finish that sentence either. The word she wanted was *violent* and it seemed like a violation of the peace in this place.

But the other two waited, until she finished her sentence.

"It was scary," she said, deciding not to go with *violent*. "I saw them on the way out."

Mr. Chester nodded, his gaze meeting Briella's. He seemed to understand what she was saying.

"I was here when they arrived," he said. "They were furious with each other. Your poor receptionist wouldn't give either of them the cremains they asked for, because apparently, there's some kind of legal battle…?"

"Oh," the owner said. "I know who they are. And yes, there's a legal battle. They're not supposed to come here in person anymore. I didn't realize…"

She closed her eyes, catching herself. Then she shook her head again, and opened her eyes, not looking any calmer.

"But that's not an excuse," she said. "We try to make your experience here as smooth as possible, and we failed that.

When we call you, we set your loved ones in a different area, alphabetically, and we—"

"It's all right," Mr. Chester said. "Really. Everyone makes mistakes."

"Yes, but this…" The owner's voice broke. "We've never had this happen before."

"And I'm sure it won't happen again," Briella said. "I used to do crisis management for businesses—" and she had hated every minute of it, which was why she quit. "—and we found that when a serious mistake happened, the business put new systems in place to make sure the mistake would never happen again."

The woman nodded, then her expression changed, becoming just a bit hooded. Her professional look, most likely.

"For what it's worth," Briella said, "I never even opened the bag. Everything here is exactly as you gave it to me."

"Me too." Mr. Chester swept his hand—also square with long fingers—toward a bag on the table. "I wasn't…I don't know." He smiled, but it was an uncomfortable smile. "I didn't…um…I don't know if I wasn't ready to face the loss of Rose or…it just didn't feel like her."

"Yes," the woman said, and it was clear from her tone that she had launched into her canned speech. "These are just reminders of loved ones."

She leaned forward and took the bag that Mr. Chester had brought as well.

"If you would like," she said, "there are family rooms in the back, if you want to wait in private. I know how hard this is."

But something in the woman's eyes said she didn't know, that this was still new.

"We have markers on each urn to ensure that the right one goes to the right family. I just need to check our system, which is also in the back. I'll take you back there, if you would like."

"I don't mind waiting here," Briella said. She really didn't want to see all of the workings of a pet mortuary. This experience had been tough enough without putting images in her head that might never go away.

"I'll stay too," Mr. Chester said, then looked at Briella. "If you don't mind…?"

"I don't mind," she said.

"It might take fifteen minutes or so," the woman said. "You might be more comfortable."

"Take your time," Mr. Chester said, and somehow managed not to sound like a man who wanted to add *and get it right*.

The woman nodded, then disappeared through that door clutching both bags.

Briella had a hunch the woman would check and double-check and go through each system as carefully as possible, before she brought the bags back out.

Mr. Chester moved to the display of urns, hands clasped behind his back. Briella sat in the chair closest to the window. The chair was on the same wall as the door that the woman had gone through. Briella did not want to watch the door, as if she were in a hurry.

She really wasn't. She worked at home now, in the quiet, and could adjust her day if she needed to. She had promised herself that she would take it easy after Rochester died, and not put pressure on anything.

After a moment, Mr. Chester sat in a chair across from her. The entry wasn't that big, so they weren't sitting far from each other.

He looked over at the reception desk, with its empty chair. "You don't think the receptionist got fired, do you?"

"I hope not," Briella said. "Everyone's allowed one mistake."

He smiled. This time the smile was soft, and suited his face. "Let's hope this doesn't get counted as two mistakes."

Briella nodded. "I'm Briella," she said. "I'm so sorry for your loss."

"And yours," he said. "I'm Marcus, by the way."

"It's nice to meet you," she said, and then realized what she had said. "Despite the circumstances."

His smile faded just a bit. "I left work to come here. No one there seemed to understand why I thought it was important to bring the bag back. They thought it could wait."

"Yeah," Briella said. "I kept thinking about someone else, wanting their pet, and not getting even the right...what do they call it?"

"Cremains," he said in a tone that suggested he didn't like the word.

"So I came right away too," she said.

"Good thing," he said. "Then we don't need to make a third trip here, not that this is a bad place."

"Exactly," she said. "When the mobile vet told me about it, I was picturing, you know, horror movie crematoriums."

With smoke coming out of the roof and a dirty trailer park

front office, a man smoking a cigarette who took the body and tossed it on a pile.

She didn't say any of that, but maybe she didn't have to, because Mr. Chester—Marcus—smiled.

"Me too." He leaned forward just a bit. "What was your cat's name?" Then he caught himself. "Cat, right?"

"Cat," she said. "His name was Rochester."

"Rochester," Marcus said. "Rose Chester." He nodded. "I can see that."

"Me, too," she said.

"Why Rochester?" he asked. "The name?"

"That's where I was living," she said, "when he showed up. In New York, not Minnesota. All my cats have New York names now."

"All?" Marcus asked. "You have other cats."

"Two," she said. "They're a bonded pair. Bronx and Brooklyn. I'm not sure they care that Rochester is gone."

He rubbed a hand on his knees, a bit nervously. "Rose didn't like other cats. Just me." He shrugged. "I suspect she would consider it a betrayal if I got a cat, even though she's gone."

"Or maybe she would want you to be happy," Briella said.

"Naw," he said. "She really wanted me to herself." He chuckled, lost in a memory. Then he sighed. "The place is quiet without her."

"It's not quiet at my place," Briella said. "Those two play a lot. But Rochester followed me everywhere. He was my shadow from the moment we met."

"Sounds like he had a lot in common with Rose," Marcus said.

"Was she jealous of you spending time with people?" Briella asked. She had heard about cats like that.

"She hated my last girlfriend," Marcus said. "Turns out, Rose was right."

Briella nodded. "Yeah, Rochester had a radar about anyone I brought home as well. I'll miss that. The two Bs don't have that kind of radar."

The woman came out of the back with two bags. They were two different shades of gray. One was slightly darker than the other. She set them on the desk.

"I was as careful as I could be," she said. "I put everything in new bags. Yours is the darker bag, Mr. Chester, but if you would like, you can go through it and make sure."

Marcus stood, and walked over to the bags. He picked up the tag on the side. Then looked inside. "It appears to be in order," he said.

"And Ms Wilder, if you want to look at yours," the woman said.

Briella stood. She didn't have to look. She knew, somehow, that bag belonged to Rochester, just as surely as she knew that the previous one hadn't.

Still, she looked at the tag and then peered inside at the pamphlets, the framed paw print, and the tiny little urn with a cat face along the top that looked nothing at all like Rochester.

"Would it make you feel better if we checked the numbers?" she asked the woman.

"No, no," she said. "I had my assistant help me. Not the receptionist you saw, but the one…"

She mercifully let that sentence trail off. Briella didn't want to know what all of the jobs were in this building.

"I don't need to double-check," Briella said, and knew better than to ask Marcus if he did. She didn't want to put pressure on him.

"This is Rose," he said and hefted the little bag as if it held the weight of a gigantic personality.

"All right," the woman said. "Again, I'm so sorry for the mixup and if you need anything from us or the next time—"

"It's fine," Briella said, not wanting to hear the end of that sentence either. It was probably something like *the next time you need our services* which was not anything she wanted to think about. Not this week. "Thank you."

"No, thank you," the woman said. "I appreciate the under-standing."

"I'm glad you cleared it up," Marcus said, and then he walked to the door. He pulled it open, letting the lovely spring sunshine inside. He held the door for Briella, and she walked through, stepping into the faint scent of roses. Only then did she realize some were blooming near the door.

Marcus followed her out. He looked at the other car in the lot, so obviously his. He was about to say something, but Briella spoke first.

"I, um…this might be odd, but would you and Rose like to get some coffee?"

He glanced at the bag as if he were checking with it. "We would love to," he said. "But I suspect Rose will remain in the car. She was never the adventurous type."

"Neither was Rochester," Briella said. "We passed a coffee shop about a mile from here. If you want…"

"I'd love some," Marcus said, "if you don't mind me boring you with Rose stories."

"Only if I can counter by convincing you how brilliant Rochester was," Briella said.

He smiled. She was beginning to like how easy his smile was and how often he was willing to share it.

"I would love to hear about Rochester," he said. "I'll follow you to the coffee shop, since I don't remember seeing it."

Something in that sentence let her know that he had been too upset to notice. Something else they shared.

"You just hit the main road and turn left," she said. "I promise I won't drive too fast."

"All right," he said, and headed to his car, carefully putting the bag with Rose into the front passenger side. When Briella saw him put the seatbelt over the bag, she knew that they had a lot more in common than the loss of a special pet.

She went to her car, and strapped Rochester in. Then she

backed out, saw that Marcus was waiting, waved, and headed down the street.

She was most of the way to the main road when she realized that the tears no longer threatened. She had no idea what would come of coffee with Marcus, and she wasn't sure that mattered, not in the long run.

But in the short run, it would be lovely to discuss Rochester with someone who understood the loss of a family member—and felt it, as deeply as she did, every single day.

For Cheepy

GOT
STEAMPUNK
MAGIC?

WorldoftheFey.com

MINIONS AT WORK
MISGUIDED MINIONS FACE HARD TIMES
Yes, it IS definitely a lighthouse! But aren't we supposed to sail AWAY from those?
I'LL HAVE MINE ON THE ROCKS!
BY J. STEVEN YORK

Hey, boss! Where's Minion Number 2? I haven't seen him around, and even his BUNK is empty. His bunk is NEVER empty!
He's on vacation in VEGAS.
Z-Z-Z-Z
-GLUG-
AGAIN? Isn't this like his THIRD vacation in three months? The guy is lazy, but this is NEXT LEVEL!

"Number 2 follows his own RULES and, as you KNOW, his own immoral code. I can't STOP him. I've certainly TRIED!"
Oh, yeah, baby! Is that a THONG or is it DENTAL FLOSS? Daddy LIKES! Also, call me DADDY!

01011010-01011010-01011010-01011010
Knowing him, he's doing something IMMORAL, DEPRAVED, or just WRONG!
He's my oldest FRIEND, but I can't endorse his behavior, especially when I'm not there to MODERATE him!

Aw, yeah! Spread that lotion around! Rub it in HARD!

01011010-01011010-01011010-01011010
He's not YOUR responsibility
But is IS! He's like a BROTH-ER to me! We go WAY back! I think the first lair we worked together was in BLACK & WHITE! I
MINION CAT!
try to keep him out of trouble, and get him out of the trouble he's already in! And in turn he -- does whatever he WANTS...
That's a sibling, alright!

Come on! Roll over, baby! I need to see those CONVEXITIES! Oh, yeah! That's right!
murr-ow?
QUANTUM TELEPORTED MINION CAT!

01011010-01011010-01011010-01011010
Las Vegas brings out the WORST in him! His RAGING misogynism! His perverse obsession with PHOTOGRAPHY!

Check it out, sweetie! I've got a BIG TELEPHOTO LENS up here! Turn around so I can ZOOM IN! And focus!
Murr-ow!
CLINK!
CLINK!
THUMP!

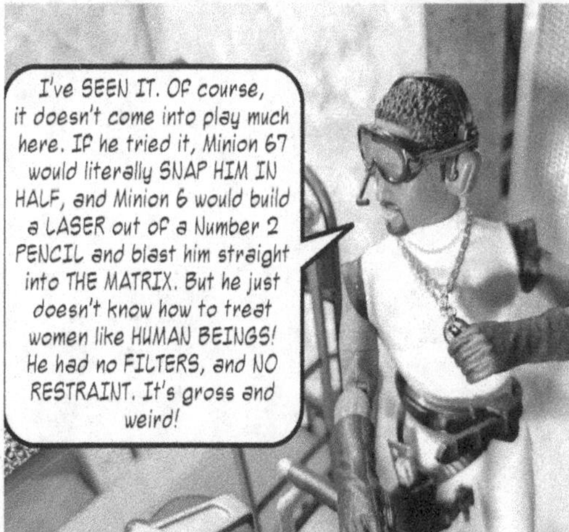

I've SEEN IT. OF course, it doesn't come into play much here. If he tried it, Minion 67 would literally SNAP HIM IN HALF, and Minion 6 would build a LASER out of a Number 2 PENCIL and blast him straight into THE MATRIX. But he just doesn't know how to treat women like HUMAN BEINGS! He had no FILTERS, and NO RESTRAINT. It's gross and weird!

Yeah! Stretch out on that lounge and I'll show you my long DEPTH OF FIELD! Let me EXPOSE you and I'll adjust your histogram and we can work on my CHROMATIC ABORATION!
Brr-row!

Look, the guy's a co-worker and all, but his transgressions shouldn't go TOTALLY unpunished! I almost wish, there could be some sort of COSMIC JUSTICE to show him the error of his ways!
Brr-row?

AYE-EEEEE!!!
(WILHELM SCREAM)
CRASH!
Purrr-purrr-purrr!

www.ingramcontent.com/pod-product-compliance
Lightning Source LLC
Chambersburg PA
CBHW010731100726
47899CB00009B/3003